BOOKS BY AVA STRONG

REMI LAURENT FBI SUSPENSE THRILLER
THE DEATH CODE (Book #1)
THE MURDER CODE (Book #2)
THE MALICE CODE (Book #3)
THE VENGEANCE CODE (Book #4)
THE DECEPTION CODE (Book #5)
THE SEDUCTION CODE (Book #6)

ILSE BECK FBI SUSPENSE THRILLER
NOT LIKE US (Book #1)
NOT LIKE HE SEEMED (Book #2)
NOT LIKE YESTERDAY (Book #3)
NOT LIKE THIS (Book #4)
NOT LIKE SHE THOUGHT (Book #5)
NOT LIKE BEFORE (Book #6)
NOT LIKE NORMAL (Book #7)

STELLA FALL PSYCHOLOGICAL SUSPENSE THRILLER
HIS OTHER WIFE (Book #1)
HIS OTHER LIE (Book #2)
HIS OTHER SECRET (Book #3)
HIS OTHER MISTRESS (Book #4)
HIS OTHER LIFE (Book #5)
HIS OTHER TRUTH (Book #6)

DAKOTA STEELE FBI SUSPENSE THRILLER
WITHOUT MERCY (Book #1)
WITHOUT REMORSE (Book #2)
WITHOUT A PAST (Book #3)

CHAPTER ONE

Michelle's feet found the slots between the train tracks, her hands spread on either side of her as if she were keeping balance. Alone, in the dark, she felt uneasy. She could feel the eyes on her. She'd spotted the three men in the construction site earlier. At first, she'd hoped they'd let her pass without incident.

But now, they were leaning against the chain fence of their job site, chuckling to each other and making comments that were best left ignored.

Especially so late. So isolated.

She continued to totter along the tracks, refusing to display fear. With these sorts, fear was like the scent of steak to a pitbull.

"Hey there, pretty!" one of them called out. "Mind giving me a twirl?"

The other two hooted like a couple of gorillas. Their fingers pressed through the mesh of the fence, their eyes wide in the dark, beneath the glare of the moon. Behind them, a couple of LED security lights illuminated the construction zone. Fluttering, orange construction tape flapped on the wind from where it was attached to traffic cones set around an open manhole.

The men were greasy, dirty. All three wearing orange vests.

"Hey, sugar!" another one said. "You look cold—let Uncle Ritchie keep you warm, hon."

She turned, flashing a middle-finger—which elicited another series of howls—and picked up the pace, still along the tracks.

As she hurried away, she glanced back. The men weren't chasing. They were still laughing, still taunting. What some might call some good old fashioned fun.

Her eyes narrowed. The sort of "fun" that would leave her terrified for months about taking this route home. Very, very fun.

But she shook her head, reaching a curve in the tracks and hopping off onto the dusty trail that ran alongside. She had problems of her own to worry about. She couldn't linger on the bad behavior of a few goons.

Their last howled comment had stung. Indeed, she wasn't warm. Nor did she really have a place to get warmth. Ahead, she spotted the trainyard she called home. Others might have just called her homeless. As she moved towards the trainyard, across the dusty path, her eyes were drawn by the glass bottles shattered at the foot of a brick wall.

How many of those bottles had she contributed? Too many. Far too many.

Her hands trembled as she stared at the glass, but she forced herself to look away. “The first step,” she mumbled to herself, “to solving a problem, is admitting you have one... Wait, no, that's not it.” She frowned, trying to remember what the AA leader had said earlier tonight. She'd been attending the group for two weeks now.

She hadn't had a sip in nearly five days. A record for her.

She reached for the metal gate which she'd left unlocked. A rusted chain wrapped around the bars, securing it to the wall. But the padlock was busted. The chain rattled as she pulled open the gate. Ahead, along the edge of old tracks, beneath a curving platform, she spotted her small tent, the cheapest kit she could find at Walmart and hardly more than a little cardboard and Styrofoam.

Home sweet home.

It would be nice to get some sleep at least.

She began to pull the chain back into place.

And that's when she heard the sound of footsteps. Chills erupted up her spine. A steady, loping gait. A jogger, she realized. Running along the path next to the train.

She glanced through the dark, making sure she was safely positioned on the other side of the locked gate. Her fingers shook as she adjusted the chain. She couldn't lock it—she'd broken the mechanism to enter the first time. But she draped the chain in such a way that it *appeared* locked.

Michelle's heartbeat kept time with the patter of approaching footsteps.

A swishing headlamp bobbed up and down as the silent runner drew nearer. She draped the chain through the bars, wrapping it around the gate, then stepped back. She shot a quick look towards her hurried bluff. It *looked* locked. Didn't it? It had lasted for nearly six months now, ever since she'd moved into the abandoned trainyard.

The less attention the better, she realized. She began turning to hastily move back through the yard.

“Hang on!” a voice suddenly called. A high-pitched, almost feminine voice.

The sound of footsteps went quiet. The bright light shone through the bars. She couldn't make out the man's face—couldn't make out his features. It was a man. That much was clear due to his sheer size. Though she couldn't make him out in the dark... he was big. *Very* big.

"Hey, Michelle!" the voice called.

The shivers spread from her neck to her arms. How did he know her name? How did he know her damn name?

"H—hello?" she said. Someone from group? Maybe she'd forgotten something—but this thought was laughable. How could she forget something? She didn't own *anything.*

Suddenly a hand grabbed at the chain. It pulled. The sound of metal clinking against metal was like the slither of a snake. She stumbled back now, quickening away.

The man didn't even hesitate. He pulled the chain off and cast it aside. She heard where it struck the smashed bottles. The gate opened slowly, creaking on rusty hinges.

"Michelle, Michelle," he murmured in a gentle voice. About an octave too high, a jarring voice. All she could really see were his hands—the only part of him extending past the bright, LED runner's headlamp. Enormous hands. He was gesturing at her to draw nearer.

Her own throat was dry. Her heart was making a bid for freedom up her neck. She stumbled over a cement curb, but caught herself against an old, moldered train car. Splinters fell; one of her fingers indented the water-damaged wooden box on wheels.

She steadied herself, shouting, "Go away! Leave me alone!"

But the jogger wasn't moving now. He'd gone still in the center of the gate, his headlight moving up and down as if he were nodding.

She pushed off the moldered train car, stumbling over metal ties, hastening towards her small shelter. Little more than a tent and cardboard. It wouldn't provide much in the way of protection, but the small three-inch blade she hid under her pillow would.

"Michelle!" the voice called after her. "How about I race you?"

"Go away!" she screamed, louder. Never before would she have imagined that she'd wanted the attention of those construction workers. But now, any witness would do. How the hell did this creep know her name?

"I'll race you!" he shouted, still standing by the gate. "If you can make it to that railroad crossing ahead of me, I'll let you live!"

Her eyes bugged. Now she was in full panic mode. She couldn't afford a phone, couldn't afford a gun. Pepper spray had been used last week on a handsy maintenance man. She was unarmed, isolated. Her knife—which she didn't take to group out of fear of being kicked out—was under her pillow. *Shit.* What did he mean *let her live*?

She broke into a sprint, racing towards her tent.

The man behind her let out a loud guffaw. And then a burst of wild movement. Thumping, rapid footfalls. Fast, faster.

Far faster than her.

She was fifteen feet from the tent. Ten.

She heard breathing, but it didn't come ragged or gasping from behind her. It was a regimented, disciplined inhalation followed by an exhalation.

She shot a wide-eyed look of panic back over her shoulder. The man was coming after her like a freight train. His body like a machine, arms moving like pistons, legs pounding the ground. He'd switched off his headlamp now. She could just make out a corded, muscled physique—a mountain of a man, hastening in her direction.

Five feet to the tent.

She sobbed, lunging towards it. Her knife was beneath the pillow. It would be there. She knew it would be there.

She hit the tent, scrambling into it. The zipper ripped, but she didn't care. He fingers darted beneath her pillow, desperately searching for her only—

Nothing.

She panicked. She skimmed her fingers across the ground, over the bed, beneath the thin foam mattress. Nothing. Nothing at all.

She spun around, one leg still jutting out of the tent flap she'd ripped through, her eyes bulging in her skull. A shadow fell across the tent. A large, hulking figure.

"Tsk, tsk," the man tutted. His high-pitched voice still sounded feminine. "Is this what you're looking for?"

She stared through the flap. Glimpsed a flash of silver. A knife dangling in her tent flap. "Now Michelle, I'm really disappointed. Also, I said I'd race you to the railroad crossing. You went the wrong direction..."

The voice was jovial, friendly. Almost like a doting mother or a playful older sister. She didn't have fond memories of such people in her life, though, so it only filled her with more horror. She tried to kick out, to knock the knife loose.

But she missed, and he caught the foot through the tent.

"Stop struggling," the man demanded, his voice going deeper, suddenly, rumbling. "Stop it—I don't want to damage you! Please, just stay still."

She screamed as loud as she could, kicking again and again.

But out here, among the junk and abandoned trains, no one would hear her except the looming shadow.

He sighed. "I really, really don't want to hurt you."

And then he tugged at her leg, pulling her bodily from the tent.

Her eyes bugged; her heart skipped. It was like she was a twig in the grasp of a tornado. She couldn't resist—the strength of the assailant was overpowering.

She tried desperately to kick, but it was like stomping at granite.

A thick hand pulled her from the tent and lifted her *bodily,* holding her upside down. She screamed, but the blood was rushing to her head, her throat constricted as she swung, staring at two, massive legs.

"I don't want to damage you, Michelle," the voice repeated, gentle again.

And then she was lifted suddenly, higher. She felt a sharp pain along her neck. A sudden warmth.

"Just calm down, honey," the voice whispered. She felt something pat her cheek in a consoling gesture. "Calm down, dear. It's all going to be okay now. I'm here to help."

The pain gave way to more panic and terror. Warmth spread from her neck, dripping along her chin. She heard a quiet tapping sound against the ground where she dangled upside down. Her vision swam, her head pounded.

And then she lost all lines of thought.

CHAPTER TWO

Dakota Steele pushed through her apartment door, phone in her hand, her brow furrowed as she listened to the final sentences of the recorded voicemail.

Things going on here... things you and Marcus never knew. Just let it go...

She shut the door behind her, phone still raised as she replayed the message for what felt like the fiftieth time.

Only a week had passed since she'd received the message, and she couldn't get it out of her head. She brushed a hand through her dirty-blonde hair, twisting the fringe to hide the streak of premature gray that threatened to dangle over her sea-gray eyes.

Dakota tossed her keys into the dish next to the door, double-checked the locks and inhaled the faint scent of fresh paint. The apartment outside Quantico was far nicer than the one she'd had back in Rapid City, but it didn't yet feel like home.

Not a chance in hell, Steele, the recorded message was saying. *"It's a dead case. Got me? Don't call again..."*

The voice of ex-Supervising Agent Drafuss blared from the speakers at full volume. Dakota had practically memorized the mini lecture but now she was trying to listen for any background noises. What had Agent Drafuss so scared?

For the last few weeks, she'd been trying to track down Drafuss's new address, but it wasn't listed, and if she tried to find him via some database, it would undoubtedly ping the old supervisor.

As Dakota's brow scrunched, a text vibrated her phone. She frowned as the voicemail was cut off mid-sentence. Her expression lightened somewhat, though, as she read the message.

From Agent Bonet—one of her old coworkers, and a mutual friend of Dakota and Marcus.

Also, a very good-looking old coworker.

The message simply read: *Heard you were back in town! We should meet up soon!*

Dakota studied the message, feeling a faint smile crease her lips. It wouldn't be so bad to grab drinks with Bonet, would it? He'd been a football player back in his youth, and still had the physique to match. The two of them had bonded over their background in athletics. Combat sports and playing linebacker for a Division I school weren't *that dissimilar.* Hell, he even had a cauliflower ear to match Dakota's.

She reached up, fingers touching absentmindedly at her injured ear.

She quickly texted back. *"Sure! Sounds good—Just let me know when!"*

She lowered the phone and gave a faint nod. Aloof but friendly. Besides, it wasn't like he was asking her on a date. Definitely not a date. He probably just wanted to know what the hell had happened three months ago, almost four now.

She'd quit the agency and moved back to Rapid City, all because of a failed case. An innocent victim was killed because Dakota had made a mistake... But Agent Drafuss's voicemail was resurrecting her curiosity. She'd never heard the man so spooked.

Dakota hesitated, frowning. In fact, Agent Bonet worked as a techie. If anyone could give her access to the old case files on the down-low, it'd be the handsome linebacker.

Besides, she smirked, it wouldn't hurt to hear his voice again.

She nodded to herself, standing near her mini- ridge, stocked with seltzer water, and gave Bonet a call. She nearly hung up twice as the phone rang, but by the sixth ring, a voice suddenly answered.

"Dakota?" the voice said, eagerly. "Hey, is that you?"

Dakota hesitated, swallowing back a lump in her throat. Again, briefly, she considered hanging up. But no—shit... he clearly knew it was her number. How else would he have texted? Besides, she needed his help...

Plus... if she was honest... one of her fears of returning to Quantico was having no friends, no allies. Marcus Clement, her partner, would certainly have her back. But already, Dakota sensed hostility from the new Supervising Agent.

Another friend, a very good-looking friend at that, could make a difference.

She let out a shaking breath, then said, "Hey Mark! It's been a while."

"Ha! I'm so glad you called. Did you get my message?"

"Umm—yeah. Yeah, just saw it. I texted back."

"Oh, woops, guess I missed it. Huh—here, let me check—"

"No, no," Dakota said hurriedly. "That's fine. We can figure out scheduling when it's convenient for you."

"No worries. I'm not doing anything, Steele." He chuckled and she could picture the way his perfect jaw and bright, baby blue eyes would look. "Just trying to look busy for the head honchos. You know how it is."

Dakota laughed uneasily. She wasn't sure the best way to ask for a favor. It felt awkward already. She didn't want Mark Bonet to think she was just trying to use him. But she could also feel her own sense of urgency.

Something about her last case had Drafuss spooked. Enough to get him fired? Relocated?

Her brimming sense of curiosity prompted her next question. "Say, Mark, I don't know what they've been chatting about around the water cooler, but I was wondering if Drafuss is around at all..."

She tried to keep her tone innocent, carefree, but even now she felt a jolt of guilt at the deception. Honesty mattered to her. Straight-shooting mattered.

But Bonet didn't seem to notice. "Drafuss? Old ballbuster is gone actually. Left about a week after you did."

"Right. Any idea where he went to?"

"Not really sure. Probably some new cushy office position. Why do you ask?"

"No reason!" Dakota said quickly. "It's—no, it's fine." She swallowed. Now came the hard part. There was no way to do it without just doing it. She bit her lip, tried to think of the best phrasing, but Marcus was the one who knew his way around words. Dakota preferred field work. She ended up blurting out, "I—I guess it's irregular, but I was wondering if I could get a copy of that case file."

"Sorry, which one?"

"*That* one," she said a bit more pointedly.

"Oh, huh," he replied. "Umm..." He trailed off and Dakota felt a sinking sensation. "Actually—you know that file is currently locked."

Dakota momentarily forgot that she wanted to make a good impression. "Locked?" she said, practically screeching it, her voice an octave higher. She swallowed, composing herself. "Sorry, I mean *locked*? How?"

She heard the sound of typing keys, a faint pause, then, "Huh. Strange. Looks like you need permission from Agent Carter."

"Wait, you mean the new boss?"

"That's the one." Bonet whistled faintly. "Hate to be the bearer of bad news, Dakota, but Supervising Agent Carter is a bit of a hard head."

I know, Dakota thought, remembering her last run-in with Carter. The woman hadn't seemed at all fond of Dakota or of allowing her to return. It had taken some convincing and a promise to attend therapy. If not for Marcus's good word, Dakota wasn't sure she would ever have been allowed back.

And now this? A file locked by the supervising agent herself?

Roadblock after roadblock. First Drafuss wanted nothing to do with her and now Carter was hiding files. But why? Had it been a mistake to fly across the country?

She'd been sober for more than a week now, but could feel her anxiety rising. She glanced towards the fridge—a knee jerk reaction. In the past, she'd found bottled comfort in that appliance.

The seltzer waters were supposed to be a substitution, but the non-alcoholic beverages were about as effective at tricking her subconscious as chewing on sunflower seeds was for a smoker.

Dakota felt a prickle of longing. Not just for her old bad habit, but for Coach Little. He'd know what to say—he always knew how to motivate his athletes.

She sighed. "Thanks, Mark. Sorry for bothering you."

"No worries—no bother. But yeah," he said, a bit too eagerly, perhaps, "about drinks—this weekend work?"

"I—I think..." She wanted to say yes. She would've said yes... but now her mind was distracted once again. Someone had sealed her case. The case that had nearly ruined everything. She thought she wanted allies... Wanted friends.

But she knew the real reason why she'd returned. To find the one that got away. The killer who was out there now, laughing at her. They called him different names while working the murders. He had targeted young women. But the name that had stuck in Dakota's mind was simply the Watcher, on account of the third eye he would paint in blood on his victims' foreheads.

She shivered as a slew of pictures rapidly flashed through her subconscious. Crime scene photos she'd tried to forget and now, given this phone call, was trying to access once more.

"You know, it's fine. I'm sure you're busy," Mark said quickly, sounding mildly disappointed. "How about you let me know what day works for you? Unless—"

"No, yeah. Yeah, that'd be great," she said quickly. "Probably the weekend. Just, I'll check, okay?"

“Sure!” he brightened once more.

“Oh, damn, Mark, sorry, I'm getting another call.”

“No worries! Good talking, Dakota. Really. It's been too long!”

Dakota smiled faintly as she switched to the new caller—an unknown number. “Hello?” she said.

“Agent Steele?” came a brusque voice that somehow communicated a scowl.

“Supervising Agent Carter,” Dakota rattled off, standing to attention even though she was alone in her apartment.

“Marcus is already here,” she said, her tone terse. “Are you near the office?”

Dakota winced. “No. I didn't think I was supposed to—”

“Well come in. We can't wait all day for you.”

“Of course. Sorry. I just thought you'd said I could take today—”

“You have a case, Steele. Hurry up.”

Agent Carter hung up. Dakota stood frozen in the middle of her small, newly painted apartment, her fingertips buzzing. A case. A new case. Agent Carter was pissed, but that was history not news.

But a case.

Shit.

Was she ready? It would be the first time stepping into a BAU headquarters after her time away. Old faces, old places...

She let out a long breath. Marcus was waiting at the office. Dammit. If not for Clement, she would have been tempted to bail right at that moment.

But Marcus had gone to bat for her. Besides, if she wasn't drinking, she needed *something* to fill that void. Solving cases, chasing bad guys always brought back that familiar buzz. And on top of it, if she did a good job, perhaps Agent Carter wouldn't be so hostile. Then maybe Dakota would have a chance of accessing those sealed files.

She sighed, turned on her heel, snatched her keys, and walked right back out the door, her stomach twisting and twirling so badly she thought she might throw up.

CHAPTER THREE

The BAU offices in Virginia were offset from the main building, occupying a smaller structure that might have resembled a quadplex if not for the metal detectors and armed guards behind the bulletproof glass doors.

Dakota's magnet-strip ID allowed her entry into the foyer, and she nodded at security as she passed through the metal detectors. It might just have been her imagination, but it felt as if the guards' nods in return were a bit stilted, their expressions cold.

She rubbed at her arms and moved towards the stairs instead of the elevators. The walk would give her some time to calm down. The movement would help her focus.

How many times, back in her fighting days, had she gone for runs before a big bout?

Something about physical exertion helped narrowed her attention. She took the stairs two at a time, hurrying up, breathing a bit more heavily than she would've liked by the time she reached the second floor.

Facing the long hall, Dakota felt a prickle of unease return. This was the first time she was actually stepping into the BAU headquarters after her time away. Everything felt... grayer, colder, darker.

Now she knew it was just her imagination.

She stared down the long hall, feeling horribly like a freshman on her first day of school. She'd dropped out of high school too, before finishing her GED.

"Dakota!" a familiar, friendly voice followed by a quick wave.

Her gaze focused, and she looked up from the long hall towards a figure standing at the end of it. A beaming, crescent smile curved the face of her giant partner, Marcus Clement. Now that they were back at the office, Marcus wore a suit and tie, but it failed to hide the very edge of the comic book t-shirt he wore underneath. At least this time it didn't have a mustard stain.

Dakota's outfit was perfectly pressed, without a visible crease. She'd brushed her hair, tastefully hiding the strand of premature gray streaking dirty blonde. Her cauliflower ear was mostly hidden by her chosen hairdo—a simple, work-efficient ponytail.

Appearances mattered in Dakota's mind. The long sleeves she wore and high-neck—not quite a turtleneck, but close—disguised the many tattoos she'd gotten in her youth and now mostly regretted. Marcus had never cared about the tattoos, though. And evidently, he didn't care about bedhead either.

His hair was disheveled, and his spectacles were streaked.

He greeted her with a grin, a quick side hug, and a single word. "Defenestration," he said.

Dakota returned the hug but quickly disentangled lest Supervising Agent Carter was nearby and looking for any signs of a lack of professionalism. "I don't know," she said. "What does it mean?"

"It means to throw someone out a window," Marcus said, grinning. Then he turned, hooking his arm through Dakota's and leading her down the hall.

Marcus liked sharing his favorite pet words with her. Not only was he a comic book nerd, but he also self-styled himself a sesquipeda—dali... daley... something. Dakota couldn't remember the word for someone who loved long words, but whatever it was, Marcus was definitely that.

With Marcus's arm hooked through hers, the faint residue of warmth from his hug, and the effect of his smile whenever he saw her, Dakota found herself feeling a bit more at ease, moving down the hall with her old partner. It was Marcus who had flown to Rapid City to bring her back to Quantico. Marcus who'd gone to bat for her with Agent Carter. And Marcus whose tip she had ignored three months ago when the Watcher, the psychopathic killer, had murdered another young woman.

"Lovely to see you in the flesh," Marcus said excitedly. "I didn't think you were coming into the office until next week."

"I wasn't," Dakota said. "But Carter wants me on this case."

Marcus shot her a look, beaming. "Wonderful. She'd mentioned I wouldn't be partnering with a rookie this time." He let out a long, satisfied sigh. "It's good to have you back, Steele."

Dakota chuckled. "Appreciate it. I'm not sure the sentiment is going to be shared."

"Oh, I wouldn't be so sure. Mark from downstairs has been asking about you." Marcus wiggled his eyebrows over his glasses.

Dakota snorted, feeling the threat of a blush before looking away. She kept her expression calm and just shrugged. She had never been comfortable expressing her emotions and far preferred keeping a lid on it whenever possible.

"I don't have all day!" a voice snapped from a few doors down the hall.

Dakota stiffened. Marcus just sighed and rolled his eyes. "Camera in the stairwell," he muttered.

Together, the two of them hastened towards a half-open door—the tinted glass marked with a golden nameplate that still read *SA Drafuss.*

Dakota stared, nudging Marcus. "Still haven't changed it?"

He shook his head. "Rumor is Agent Carter is only here on a trial run. Acting supervisor. Nothing permanent yet."

Dakota frowned, thinking back to the strange voicemail she'd received from their previous supervisor. She hadn't shown Marcus the message yet. Hadn't had the time. And now certainly wasn't the opportunity.

The door pushed open, and the two of them stepped into the supervisor's office.

"Come in! Sit down," a voice said curtly. A rasping, articulate voice, like that of a particularly stern librarian.

A woman with short-cut, white hair above dark, smooth skin was sitting behind a walnut desk. The windows in the room, Dakota noticed, were all tinted or covered. She noticed a vent above the desk had been closed and taped off. Instead, a small space heater and a miniature table fan sat on the walnut desk.

The desk, she noticed, had been moved from the spot it had previously occupied, and now centered the room, sitting smack-dab in the middle of the carpeted floor. Dakota also noticed two cameras above the desk with blinking red lights. A second later, she spotted a hidden camera in a large bookcase, concealed in the binding of a particularly large almanac. The small, glass eye wouldn't have been noticed except for the conspicuous blind spot created by the visible cameras, suggesting Dakota would find a third.

Dakota cataloged all of this dispassionately in a matter of seconds. She remained straight postured, standing in the doorway at attention. Her gaze flicked back towards Supervising Agent Carter. The pale-haired woman looked quite small sitting behind such a large desk. Her dark eyes held a hint of kindness, but her steely expression quickly dissuaded any notion of hugs or kisses from the agent in charge.

"Clement, Steele," Carter rattled off. She peered at them over the desk. Two chairs sat in front of the table, but she made no indication towards them, so Dakota and Marcus maintained their standing position by the door.

"Agent Carter," Marcus said, bobbing his head in greeting. "How are you?"

She glanced towards Marcus, and her icy expression melted somewhat. She smiled, her cheeks dimpling, and she nodded, "Fine, Clement. Doing fine. How about yourself?"

"Wonderful," Marcus replied, beaming. "I checked that parking spot yesterday—the van checks out. It's a maintenance vehicle for the office complex."

"Oh, good—good," she nodded, folding her hands. "One can never be too careful," she said. "Did you tell them they can't park overnight?"

"Yes. They'll move by noon."

"Perfect."

Dakota did her best not to glance at the tinted windows, the extra cameras, or the odd placement of the desk. She'd met paranoid agents before, as well as overly cautious ones. There was a fine line between careful and crazy.

Now, though, wasn't the time to pry into the supervisor's sense of self-protection.

Almost as if she'd sensed Dakota's thoughts, Carter glanced at her, and her expression hardened once more. "Agent Steele, glad to see you could make it to work today." She didn't allow Dakota to respond before continuing, "Have you been compliant with drug-testing and mandated therapy?"

She didn't even blink as she said it. Dakota shifted uncomfortably, but just as quickly covered herself by nodding a single time. "Yes, ma'am." Marcus didn't so much as glance her way.

"Keep it up then," Carter said with a sniff. "The agency is counting on you. Now," she said, unfolding her hands and pressing them to the top of the table, "We've got two dead in the suburbs of Chicago."

"Victim type?"

"Two women," Carter said, frowning as if she took this part personally. "A college student taken from campus and a homeless woman attacked near an old train yard."

"MO?" Dakota asked.

Carter looked at her, but then seemed to decide there was no reason to be annoyed at the question and answered, "Both killed by having their throats slit. Also, they were posed."

"Posed how?" Marcus asked, frowning.

In answer, Agent Carter reached for her computer and spun it towards the agents. "The case file is in your inbox, Clement. Steele, your clearance is being reinstated but it might take a few days."

Dakota would have been disgruntled by this announcement if she hadn't been distracted by the horrible images on the computer screen. At first, it was difficult to pick out the body in the first image on account of the piles of old vehicles and rusted automobiles behind her. There were stacks of dilapidated appliances and the like. It took Dakota a second to realize she was staring at a scrapyard.

She shifted uncomfortably, leaning in before going still.

A woman was dangling upside down with chains wrapped around her ankles. Her hands were encased in metal which—Dakota stared, trying to make sense—had been welded to one of the refrigerators, as a sort of base for a grotesque sculpture. The chains around her legs extended above and were hooked onto the end of a crane. Strangely, there were tree branches bonded to the crane's hook as well, spread out in both directions.

"Bizarre," Marcus muttered.

Dakota nodded slowly. Her gaze was drawn to the second image. This time, a woman's upper body was encased in a metal sheath that spread out to form what could only be described as two wings. Bat-like, metal wings spread above her. The body was suspended by three metal legs holding the woman in a posture as if she were flying over a junk pile.

Dakota gave a faint, bemused shake of her head. "Is he posing them in junkyards?"

"The first one, yes," Carter said, nodding. "The second is in a trainyard that also is used for scraps. Those branches in the first image were welded by metal couplings to the hook."

"Welded?" Marcus said, quirking an eyebrow. "Odd. How did he get up there? No less with welding tools?"

"That," said Agent Carter, "is precisely why we're sending you two. We need to find out who is behind this, why they're posing the victims in this fashion, and we need to find out quickly. Any questions?"

Marcus raised a hand and said, "The coroner reports are emailed also?"

"Everything is in your inbox," she said.

"Then no more questions," Marcus replied.

Dakota shifted uncomfortably, staring at the images on the computer. Already, she could feel a rising sense of unease. This wasn't an ordinary killer. The posing was bizarre, but far more chilling, in Dakota's opinion, was the sheer amount of time the killer had taken to weld the metal sculptures, to pose the victims. Almost... almost like an artist going the extra mile to complete their piece.

The killer had nerves of... well, *steel,* if he was willing to risk being caught just to put the finishing touches on his grotesque sculptures. Junkyards weren't exactly public spaces, but they had employees, visitors, and offered the opportunity at being discovered.

Evidently, though, judging by the images, the killer didn't care. He was bold. Brash. Two bodies within thirty-six hours. He was moving *fast.* No reason to think he was ready to stop now. Which meant he was only just getting started.

Dakota glanced towards Agent Carter, deciding now wasn't a good time to ask for permission to access the old case files. Clearly, she still had some proving to do. But while they'd gotten off on a bad foot, Dakota felt that solving this case would go a long way in earning some leeway.

"And you?" Agent Carter said, looking towards Dakota. Her tone was less harsh all of a sudden, and some of that lingering kindness in her gaze came to the surface. "Any questions?"

"I—just the one," Dakota said. "When does our plane leave?"

CHAPTER FOUR

Dakota adjusted her tray, clicking it into place. She made sure her seat was upright and shot a sidelong glance at Agent Clement. Marcus had brought his own snacks for their flight, and the small bag of fruit gummies littered the gray folding table. He also leaned back in their economy seat, giving himself ample room for his ample frame.

He'd unbuttoned his suit and had yet to notice the gummy that had landed on his belly. The two of them took completely different approaches to air travel.

Marcus adjusted the screen of his computer and clicked through the crime scene photos, his expression of distaste growing with each image.

"Bizarre," he muttered. "Truly odd."

Dakota was no longer paying attention to the murder scenes, but rather was paying closer attention to the images *beneath* the crime scene photos—these ones displayed the driver's licenses of the victims.

Michelle Stanton, the second victim, had been in her early twenties, but had no listed home address currently. The address on the license was currently occupied by an older Korean couple with work visas. According to the locals on the scene, Michelle had been homeless.

Dakota's gaze flicked to the image of the first victim. A bright faced, smiling younger woman with vibrant eyes and dark hair. Caitlynn Jackson had been an honor roll student from a wealthy family.

"It doesn't match," Dakota murmured, shaking her head softly.

"What's that?" Marcus glanced over and the fruit gummy tumbled from his belly onto his lint-covered seat. "Oh, bonus!" he said, grabbing the red candy and popping it into his mouth.

Dakota shook her head. "The victims don't match. Different heights, different ages, different races, different socio-economic backgrounds. What's he targeting?"

Marcus frowned, glancing down at the driver's licenses. "Huh. Good point. See, that's why I bring you along, Steele. Details like that."

Dakota snorted. "Don't pretend you hadn't already noticed."

Marcus shrugged. But she noticed he didn't deny it. Still, she wasn't offended—she knew her partner was trying his best to help her feel comfortable and accommodated. As Dakota stared at the images of the two young women, both of them a decade her junior, she felt a familiar sense of anger rising in her chest.

It started as a prickle but spread as heat across her chest and arms. Both women had been vulnerable, defenseless when they'd been attacked. The killer preyed on the young and the marginalized. In one case, a college student far from home, walking towards her dorm room late at night. In the other, a homeless woman struggling to get her feet back under her.

Michelle in particular caught Dakota's attention. Coach Little, thanks to his Catholic roots, in between expletives and complaints about the boxing circuit, occasionally had some, as they called it in the sporting world, old-head wisdom to offer. Now, she remembered an expression he'd once shared. *There, but for the grace of God, go I.*

She sighed, staring at Michelle's image on the screen, wondering how much of Dakota's own life might have turned out different if not for Coach Little. If not for his hundreds of hours of investment in her. When she'd dropped out of school and ran away from home, he'd given her a place to stay. She'd slept on the old Irishman's house more than once. She'd gotten in with the wrong crowds too. Had made a bit of a mess of it. But fighting had saved her life.

Coach Little had saved her life. Not that she thanked him often enough.

Dakota couldn't help but wonder what a woman like Michelle could have done if someone, anyone, had just shown her a little bit of compassion.

Her hand balled on her lap, but she unclasped it quickly before Marcus could notice.

No one had been there for this woman while she'd been alive. It was a very poor consolation, but Dakota was determined to bring some sense of justice to an otherwise cruel ending.

It wouldn't change anything. It wouldn't help Michelle. If Coach Little had been here, she might have asked him to throw up a prayer or two on behalf of the second victim.

But Dakota and Marcus's job was of a far less ethereal and more proximate variety. They were going to catch the murderer, and they wouldn't need the wrath of the divine. No, Dakota's rage would be more than enough.

Normally, she medicated the anger with alcohol. But now she was determined to deal with the pain another way. She would make the bad guys suffer instead.

"Excuse me," a flight attendant said, smiling from the aisle at them both. "Drinks?"

Dakota blinked, glancing in surprise at the drink cart. Her eyes darted along the miniature bottles of alcohol stacked in neat trays that had been slid into the side of the cart.

"Just water, please," Marcus interrupted, raising a hand and smiling genially. "Thank you."

"And you?" the flight attendant asked, turning her smile towards Dakota.

"Umm, yeah, water. Thanks—sparkling if you have it."

Dakota didn't glance at Marcus. But she felt another flash of gratitude. She knew he sometimes got nervous on flights and, in the past, would often order some manner of small chemical courage; but now, out of solidarity, he was forgoing his coping mechanism.

As the waters were placed in their cupholders, Dakota shot a look towards Marcus. "Thanks," she muttered.

"Don't know what you mean," he replied. He tapped a finger against his computer screen while he took another sip. "See this? The second crime scene—the one where he posed the victim as if she was flying—he soldered the metal. It was quick work, but not sloppy."

"What are you saying?"

"I'm saying," Marcus replied, "that I think our killer might have experience in metalworking. It's worth keeping in mind."

Dakota studied the pictures Marcus indicated. Loops of steel soldered to rusted iron. Lengths of rebar melted against a refrigerator's lid. An odd, half-melted, metallic mess. And yet, in a horrible way, beautiful. Even the victims, how they'd been posed, seemed completely intentional. Not just intentional, but *care*ful. The bodies meant something to the killer. Almost as if he'd dealt more tenderly with them after death than before.

Dakota shuddered at the thought and reached down to take a sip of her sparkling water as the plane carried them towards their destination.

CHAPTER FIVE

As their taxi carried them towards the ten-foot, red brick wall, Dakota could feel her nerves returning. She managed to keep her emotions in check, though, as she thanked the driver, paid him, then joined Marcus on the curb to face the wall encircling their second crime scene.

She nodded, pointing against the gray skyline. "Crane," she said.

Marcus followed her indicating finger and frowned. "I see it," he murmured. He shot her a look. "The body is at the coroner's, but they left the metal sculpture intact."

The two of them approached a metal gate where two police officers stood next to a parked cruiser.

"How's it goin'?" Marcus called out, raising a hand. The cops eyed the giant with skeptical expressions.

"You feds?" one of them asked.

Dakota nodded. Marcus flashed a thumbs up along with his badge.

The cops stepped aside, glancing back towards the yard. "Isn't pretty in there," an older, grizzled officer said, shaking his head and sighing. "Not pretty at all."

"They moved the body, right?" Marcus replied, frowning. "It's been eight hours."

"Yeah, yeah—we moved it," the old-timer said. "But no way to get the blood stains out of the lime. Or the rust. There's a torture device dangling from the crane. See it?"

Dakota looked past the officer and frowned. As Marcus made small talk, as he was the sort to do, Dakota gave a hurried apology and scooted past the men, moving into the trainyard. The coroner and paramedics were gone. The body was also gone.

But the remnants of the crime scene were all too obvious. Stray gravel crunched underfoot as she craned her neck, peering up at the dangling chain from the crane hook. In the images, the corpse had been hung upside down, the chain wrapped around her ankles.

The killer was helping the woman to elevate... Why else would he have gone to the trouble to pose her so high up. Dakota also noticed an old, rusted train on overgrown tracks, just beneath the floating body.

"So that's how he reached it," she murmured.

She noticed blood stains on the metal... but not much. She frowned, glancing at the ground and looking along the old train yard. She spotted an ancient office-building with busted windows and a missing door. There were a couple more abandoned cars with paneling gone or tracks stolen.

She also spotted a tent just beneath an arching bridge.

She turned her back on the crime scene and began moving towards the tent. Someone had marked out the spot with yellow tape.

And now, as she drew nearer, stepping into the shadows of the over-arching structure, she frowned. So that's where most the blood had gone. The ground was dark—a rusted hue among the stones and dappling old, worn cardboard. The tent was ripped, torn. More blood there, too.

She glanced back towards the train. The killer had taken his victim here. Had she been sleeping? At the very least it looked as if she'd put up one hell of a fight.

Instantly, Dakota felt a flash of satisfaction.

She'd often thought that if she went down by some bad guy that she at least wanted the chance to get in a punch and a kick or two.

"Anything?" Marcus called out.

Dakota turned and shrugged. "He killed her here but posed her there. Only a short distance away."

Marcus followed Dakota's indicating finger then nodded. "Guess so."

"Why?"

"Why what?"

"Why pose her over there?"

Marcus frowned, considering the question. "You think it was pre-planned?"

"Maybe... he would've had to know Michelle beforehand, then. She wasn't random if he planned it."

"I mean... look at that thing," Marcus said, nodding towards the metal chain. "He definitely was prepared. Used a darn blowtorch by the looks of things."

Dakota felt a tinge of nostalgia at the word *darn.* Around Coach Little and most of her neighbors back home, the idea that swearing was anything but a mode of expression never would have crossed their minds. But Marcus avoided cussing, though he often reacted like a giggling schoolboy when others did it around him.

She shook her head. “So if it was planned, then he came prepared. Which means he had tools and scraps in a truck or car somewhere. Think we can get local traffic footage?”

Marcus nodded. “I'll put in a request.”

Dakota glanced back towards the broken tent, the blood stains. She shook her head. “Something else... Michelle fought.”

“Good for her.”

“I was thinking the same. But not only that—look at the blood. The tent.”

“Definitely didn't go quietly.”

Dakota nodded, but then tapped her phone. “On those images you sent, the coroner's, did you notice anything strange about the body?”

Marcus hesitated but then nodded. “Yeah. No wounds except the death blow.”

“Exactly. Almost as if the killer was trying *not* to harm her.”

“You know, except for the whole murder business,” Marcus said distastefully.

“Yeah, but you know what I mean. The bodies—they seem to matter to him. He took care not to inflict too much damage. Then he posed the body afterwards.”

“Posed it high up,” Marcus pointed out, indicating the dangling metal chain once more.

“High up,” Dakota said. “Exactly.” She frowned now, considering the implications. Why was the killer protecting the corpse? There had been no sign of sexual assault. No sign of cannibalism. Nothing she might normally have expected from such behavior.

Dakota stood in the shadows of the bridge, staring at the bloody tent and frowning.

A loud voice suddenly jarred them from their reverie. “Hey, you two—what are you doing there?”

Dakota turned sharply, instinctively lowering her center of gravity. But just as quickly she readjusted, standing straight. To anyone without training it would just have looked like a little bouncing motion as she turned.

The man walking towards them, though, scowled, moving with a limp and walking with a wooden cane. He wore a cap, with bristles of white hair jutting out from beneath. A long, curling goatee tickled the end of his sharp chin.

“This is private property!” the old man snapped. “Cops will have your hide!”

"We are the cops," Dakota replied softly.

"FBI," Marcus added, raising his badge.

The old man suddenly straightened, blinking in surprise. "Oh—oh... Right. Apologies."

"I'm Marcus Clement," Dakota's partner said, nodding in a congenial manner. "Mind sharing your name?"

"Yes, of course. Mickey Faber. I'm the manager of this place."

"This place has a manager?" Dakota said, wrinkling her nose.

Marcus cleared his throat. "I—ah, think what my partner means is this place looks like a bit of a hassle to manage all by yourself."

"I manage the scrap," he replied curtly, clearly not at all offended by Dakota's initial comment. "Trying to get the whole place dismantled by the end of the year before demolition comes through." He flashed a yellow grin. "Almost at a healthy profit just by tearing the whole place down, you know."

Marcus nodded, looking sufficiently impressed.

Dakota, though, said, "If you manage this place, did you know Michelle Stanton?"

He hesitated now, scratching at his bristly chin. Standing in the shadows of the bridge to nowhere, he looked older now, his face cast in darkness. He let out a little sigh. "I knew Michelle. Didn't know her last name was Stanton. First I heard she was here was last month. I manage a few condemned properties. I don't normally visit, except to help scrappers in."

"But you knew Michelle was staying here?"

He winced, glancing past the FBI agents towards where the cops remained by the gate. "It—it wasn't meant to be a problem. I told her she had to find another place. But... she seemed so desperate. Told me it was safer for a woman to live behind a lock," he shrugged, waving towards the walls and the gates. "To be honest, she didn't harm the place. Just sort of slept here. A pretty lady like that, I felt it was the least I could do. Can you imagine a good-looking gal trying to shack up under a bridge somewhere?" He shook his head, clicking his teeth together.

Dakota frowned. "The way you say it, it almost sounds like Ms. Stanton was expecting trouble."

The man snorted. "A young woman like that, living on the streets? Expect it or not, trouble finds you. She was just trying to stay safe. I didn't see the harm in it." He glanced up at the crane and winced. "Bad way to go. Wish I'd installed some cameras. I was going to, you know. I thought about it—but just didn't get around in time." He shook his head in disgust and heaved another sigh.

"So you can't think of anyone specific who Michelle had a problem with? Anyone she might have been scared of? An abusive ex? A stalker?"

Mickey wrinkled his nose and shook his head. "Can't say anything like that comes to mind..." He trailed off, then clicked his fingers against the curve of his walking cane. "Now that you mention it, though, one of our contracted custodians has had problems with the homeless in the yard in the past."

Dakota and Marcus both perked up now, paying attention. Mickey's brow wrinkled in consideration. "Actually, the guy I'm thinking of got into a bit of an argument with Ms. Stant—what was it? Stand?"

"Stanton."

"Yes, Ms. Stanton. He got into an argument with her last month when he found her. That's when I was brought in. I just... didn't have the heart to make her move. I told her to," he added quickly. "For legal reasons... But as for enforcing it..." He trailed off and shrugged.

"It was on the docket," Marcus added helpfully.

"Exactly." He tapped his long nose. "On my to-do list, for certain."

"This custodian," Dakota said, "his job was to keep the place clean, I imagine?"

"Clean, locks checked, mold checked—infestations managed. He advised a few months ago to hire an exterminator. You know, damn rats."

"And this custodian had an altercation with our victim only a few weeks ago?"

"Month ago, but yeah. Guess that's a few weeks."

Dakota frowned. "Does this man have a name?"

"Sure. He isn't one of my employees. He's Alec Haines. Actually, the little redneck is scheduled to work at one of my garages in the depot across the street." Mickey gave a nasty little chuckle. "Bastard's been lying on his timecard. You can tell him I sent you."

Dakota was already turning. Marcus took the time to thank the trainyard manager before falling into step behind her. As they moved, Dakota couldn't help but glance at the metal *thing* and the horrible backdrop.

A trainyard of all places... Why?

The isolation? Perhaps... but it also gave any manner of a potential weapon or hiding place the chance of being spotted. She would've assumed there were cameras on site if she hadn't seen it during the day.

So why had the killer chosen *this* location in particular? Would Alec Haines have the answers she needed?

She picked up her pace, moving over old rail ties, and along grease-stained concrete and asphalt with a skip in her step.

"That one!" Mickey called. "See the big sign?"

Dakota nodded. "Saw it on the way in."

Marcus gave another wave to the cops as they swept past, moving onto the sidewalk and then hastening across the cracked and broken asphalt towards the garage across the street.

CHAPTER SIX

The train depot across the road had a far newer, corrugated metal fence. Two security cameras sat on top of metal posts. The garage next to the depot had three doors, two of them open, displaying large bays with maintenance and construction vehicles being tended to.

Dakota's eye was caught by a shower of sparks in one corner of the garage as a man in a protective helmet worked on a vehicle that resembled a dozer with a big rolling attachment on the front. Dakota wasn't an expert in construction but she guessed this was used for smoothing fresh asphalt.

Another mechanic was working on a small golf cart with tool buckets in the back seat. No sparks flew from this particular vehicle, but the man cursed every couple of seconds as he tried to plug a leak in the front of the cart, evident by the pool of oil spreading across the slick ground or staining the hems of his sleeves.

Marcus allowed Dakota to take the lead as she entered the garage, shielding her face against the sparks from the man working on the dozer. Once there was a lull in the sound of auto shop work, she raised her voice, and called out, "Is Alec Haines here?"

At first, it seemed as if her words hadn't registered. But then, the man who was trying to juggle oil, and the one with the protective face mask, both lowered their tools, and looked in her direction.

"Who's asking?" called the man with the mask.

"FBI," Dakota countered. "Are you Alec?"

The man with the blowtorch looked uncomfortable now. He wore thick, protective gloves, and the large mask covering his face gave him an ominous air.

He shifted uncomfortably by the large wheel of the vehicle he was working on. "FBI?" he said tentatively, shooting an uncomfortable look towards his coworker. "This isn't about the homeless lady across the street, is it?"

"Michelle Stanton," Dakota said. "It is." She couldn't help but notice the blowtorch. Her heart quickened. While he was a custodian across the street, it looked as if he also moonlighted as a repairman of some sort.

She hesitated, glancing towards Marcus. The agent raised a placating hand. "We just have a few questions Mr. Haines."

"I didn't say I was Haines," the man retorted, slowly rising from where he crouched and gripping his blowtorch like a club.

"Are you?" Marcus said.

The man adjusted his face-shield, shifting from foot to foot. "You didn't say what this was about..."

"We told you," Marcus replied, jutting a thumb over a shoulder. "Michelle Stanton. Sir, could you please lower the torch?" Marcus's hand moved slowly, cautiously towards his holster on his hip. He left it there, hovering, not pulling his weapon but implying.

Dakota watched as the welder swallowed and began to shift nervously back. "I didn't have nothin' to do with that!" he said.

"That's fine, sir—please, lower the torch." Marcus took a step forward.

This, however, the man seemed to take as more of a suggestion than directive. He held it nervously, his head swiveling, glancing between the two of them. "I hear she was stabbed—that true? I never stabbed no one in my life."

"Who told you she was stabbed?" Dakota said, frowning.

He glanced at her now from behind his mask. "I—what?" He took a shuffling step back but knocked over a box of tools, sending screwdrivers and wrenches and the like scattering across the cold, concrete floor. The sound of rattling metal faded only to be replaced by rapid and panicked breath.

"Sir," Marcus admonished, "please, we just need you to—"

But one look at the big agent, and the man in the mask cursed, threw his tool on a workbench and then spun on his heel, sprinting for the exit in the back of the building.

Dakota shouted, hotfooting after him, "Stop! Put your hands up!"

But their suspect wasn't in a compliant mood. He slammed through the exit, stumbling out into an alley and hurtling down dark cement, racing towards a busy street.

Marcus yelled, "I'll go around!"

Dakota was already breaking through the emergency door. The fire alarm was now ringing above them in ear-splitting yodels. A couple of other employees, further in the office, emerged. She still hadn't confirmed the masked man was their suspect but evidenced by the way he was reacting, she surmised it was a good bet.

She raced after him, sprinting down the side alley towards the busy street. The man paused on the sidewalk, looking one way, then the other. He cursed, and sprinted to the right, in the direction of the other trainyard.

Dakota lost sight of him. A few seconds later, followed by the sound of her own thumping footsteps, and huffing breaths, she heard a sharp yelp and a loud *thud*.

Breathing heavily, sweat prickling her brow, as she rounded the edge of the building, she spotted where Agent Clement and the welder were locked in a wrestling match.

After the unfortunate shooting of the suspect on their previous case, Marcus seemed reluctant to pull his firearm. And now he was rolling on the cement, trying to get the upper hand over his attacker.

It would've been easy, except for the two-inch penknife the welder gripped in his hand. He was shouting, "You can't take me back! I won't go back!"

The knife was so small that Dakota thought Marcus might be able to just rip it from the assailant's hands. Clement was playing it cautious, though, holding the fellow's wrist and trying to twist his arm.

In the meantime, she realized he was just stalling, waiting for backup. For her. She raced up behind the struggling men, and shouted, "Hands up, now."

The man panicked. He let out a yelp and tried to slice at Marcus in his desperation.

Dakota cursed, despite Clement being within earshot. She didn't have a clean angle. So she rapidly holstered her firearm and then snagged the man's wrist. She slid her arm underneath the man's back and locked her forearm beneath the man's neck. The motions were smooth, taking only as long as thought. She moved to the tiger claw position, using the man's shoulder. Marcus still maintained his grip but was desperately trying to pry the knife free.

The man tried to shout more, but Dakota slipped her arm around his neck, executing a rear naked choke. Messy, since she didn't have him in a back mount, but the welder was hardly a trained fighter. He didn't put up much resistance.

"Drop the knife!" Dakota shouted in his ear, pulling him bodily off Marcus and holding him on top of her, both of them facing towards the sky.

The man tried to speak, but his voice came strangled from her grip. His hands jutted upwards, and the small penknife clattered to the sidewalk. Marcus pushed them both off to the side but was careful not to shove either Dakota or the assailant too hard. Clement even paused long enough to dust the welder's sleeves. He said, "There was no need for that." He bent over, took the penknife, folded it, and slipped it into his big pocket. "You can have this back after we've had you answer a few questions."

Dakota wasn't nearly so optimistic about the prospects of returning the man's blade. She loosened her grip a bit and said, into his ear, “No more stabbing, got me? I'm going to let you up now.”

He was still wearing his stupid mask. He kept shaking his head and shouting, "You can't take me back. I won't go!"

She slipped out from under him, still controlling his head, then turned him sharply and reached out to slip his mask off.

It revealed a young man's face, with pimples, and a prematurely receding hairline.

He was breathing heavily, sweat slicking his face. He had a couple of burn marks under his chin, and a long scar over one eye. He was shaking his head still, sending droplets of sweat flying. "Please. I didn't do anything! I'm innocent!"

Dakota frowned, and said, "Normally innocent people wait until they're accused before declaring their innocence. Alec, you're coming with us."

She twisted his hands behind his back in a deft movement that reminded her of the first motion for a triangle choke, and then she locked his hands. As the cuffs *clicked* into place, she glanced at Marcus. "Think you could call a squad car?"

He breathed heavily, wiping daintily at his sweaty forehead. He then flashed a thumbs-up, and pulled his phone from his pocket.

CHAPTER SEVEN

Marcus tried to settle in the interrogation room chair, but they always made these metal seats so darn small. He felt uncomfortable as he shifted to the left, then the right, trying to find a position most amenable to his ample frame. In the end, he opted for standing, pushing the chair back beneath the table which was bolted to the ground. The chair legs scraped against the concrete, and he winced apologetically as both Dakota and Mr. Haines looked up at him.

Mr. Haines's expression was a mixture of shock and fear and fury. His emotions played in equal parts across his countenance and also in the way he chose to communicate with them. Dakota, on the other hand, had an expression like a professional poker player. She always knew how to play her cards close to the vest.

Marcus wasn't nearly so close-guarded. He found himself tapping a finger against his upper thigh, his own nerves at an all-time high. Not due to the case, though he was focused on solving it. But because he wanted this all to work out.

He shot another look towards Dakota as she read through a report on the table in front of her. The silence lingered in the room a moment longer as Dakota forced their suspect to wait. She had a bit of a vengeance streak for suspects that assaulted... well... *him.* Dakota was nothing if not protective.

Which was one of the reasons he was so excited to be working with her again. He'd missed her. Missed having her at his back. It just wasn't the same, after nearly a decade together, trying to work with the rookies Agent Carter kept pairing him with.

And so far... his instincts were proving correct.

Dakota had noticed the lack of damage to the corpses. She'd noticed the differences in the victim-type. She had an eye for that sort of thing which had made a bit of a name for her at the BAU before the *incident.*

Not only that, though, she'd also managed to stop the suspect from attacking him. She even looked sober. He shot her another look, but then caught himself, deciding that if he wasn't careful, she'd notice his attention and read his mind in that way she so often did.

Dakota was settling now, clearing her throat and looking up from the folder with a cocked eyebrow. "So, Mr. Haines," she began after having let him sweat for nearly five minutes, "you have a bit of an arrest record, I see."

She looked up, blinking in the bright lights above the reflective table. Alec Haines shifted uncomfortably, frowning at them from beneath his sloping forehead. He had young features, but according to his license, he was in his thirties.

"I wasn't violating my parole," he snapped, reflexively. "Shit, I have a job. I've been clean for like five months. You've got nothing on me!"

Dakota closed the folder slowly, nodding as she listened. "I see," she said. "Assault is a pretty serious charge. So is domestic abuse. Do you enjoy hitting women, Mr. Haines?"

He scowled at Dakota. "I can think of one I'd like to—"

"Watch it!" Marcus snapped.

The man shifted uncomfortably and shot the agent a reproachful look. He tried again. "I made some mistakes—I paid my debt. I didn't have anything to do with that broad getting strung up."

"So you know about Ms. Stanton's death."

"Everyone knew, lady. She was, like, the local homeless hottie. Couple of the guys at the shop tried to take videos through the bars.

"You didn't?"

"Nah, no. Parole officer sometimes goes through my damn phone. Like I said, I ain't going back."

Dakota frowned. "You probably should've thought of that before trying to stab my partner."

Marcus crossed his arms, preferring to let his partner take the lead on this one. Normally, Dakota liked to keep quiet in interviews, but he could tell she was making an effort. Not just to prove herself to him, but to prove what she was capable of to herself. After the last case with the Motorcycle Killer, Dakota had regained the *itch.* The urge. Some people caught bad guys out of a sense of duty. Marcus focused on helping the survivors, the victims. But Dakota... she was different. She saw it as her job to put killers behind bars. Some people had a chip on their shoulder, others had skeletons in their closets. Dakota had both. At least this way, sitting across from a murder suspect, her jaw slightly clenched, her gaze fixated, she wasn't medicating in more damaging ways.

Dakota continued pressing. "We heard you had an altercation with the victim before. Is it true you work custodial shifts across the street from your depot?"

The man snorted, shrugging. "So what? I gotta pay the bills some way. Besides, just because I yelled at some lady bum doesn't mean I killed her."

"Michelle," Dakota said, enunciating the name clearly, "got in your way, is that it? You didn't want her on the premises, so you decided to do something about it when the manager didn't."

"No—no nothing like that." He was pale faced, perspiring like a faucet. "You can't pin that on me!"

"I'm not pinning anything," Dakota said. "You're guilty as sin. Why else did you run?"

"I didn't run!"

"Mr. Haines, I was there, remember. So was my partner here. You pulled a knife on a fed, and you fled your workshop. Why?"

Haines muttered beneath his breath, shaking his head ferociously. "I'm not going back," he kept saying. "Not going back."

Dakota leaned across the table. Marcus wasn't sure she'd blinked yet in the entire exchange. "Alec," Dakota said, "This doesn't look good for you. Michelle was posed—her body was posed. Whoever did it has metalworking skills. Soldering, extruding, forging. The sorts of skills you possess."

"What? I'm no metalworker, lady. I can use a blowtorch in a pinch for some fixes. That's about it. Besides, I'm telling you, I didn't kill anybody."

"You have to do better than that," Marcus said, speaking up for the first time in a while.

Their suspect winced, his eyes bouncing between the two of them like ping-pong balls. "I didn't," he squeaked. "I... I'm not going back." He swallowed, nibbling on the corner of his lip.

Marcus could tell a snitch when he saw one. The man was about to spill his guts. Dakota seemed to sense it too, just like the old days. Both of them in sync, both of them picking up on the same clues.

They waited in silence, allowing Haines to fill in the blanks with his own imagination. Nothing could be more tormenting than an unsettled mind's own whispers.

At last, he let out a long breath and said, still in that squeaking voice, "I didn't kill shit. I had nothing to do with that tramp. Didn't like her. She smelled. Her tent smelled. It got in the way. Sue me. I had a bad day, yelled at her, and she chucked a bottle at my head."

Dakota blinked. "She attacked you?"

“Yeah, lady! Just ask the manager. Guess Mickey didn't tell you that part, huh? Asshole still complaining about those timecards?”

“Focus,” Dakota said.

“I *am* focused. It's you and the jolly giant over there that need some resetting, lady. Look I ran. Sure. Of course I ran. I had to run. Not my damn fault I was stuck working on a stolen dozer.”

Dakota blinked, leaning back in her chair, and crossing her arms. “Excuse me?”

Now that he'd chosen to spill the beans, Mr. Haines was all too forthcoming. He snorted and shook his head, sending some sweat droplets flicking across the room. “Stolen milling machine,” he said. “Couple of the guys at the shop bring ‘em in. We take the parts we like, ship the rest. Easy cash. I thought that's why you were there at first. I panicked. Didn't want to be standing around with a big ol’ miller in the shop. Especially not while I was working on it.”

Marcus leaned in, peering across the table. “You're saying you ran because you were working in a chop shop for heavy machinery?”

He looked at Marcus, forcing a quick smile. “I mean, come on man. It's kinda funny, yeah?”

“You tried to stab me.”

“It was a mistake.”

“Yes. Yes, it was.” Marcus leaned back, shooting Dakota a sidelong glance.

“Damn it, man. I didn't kill anyone!” Alec protested louder. “You can't send me back. I can't do it. Please!”

Dakota sighed, shaking her head. “I'm not sure how you think working in a chop shop meets the terms of your parole.”

“Lady, I just told you I didn't kill anyone, though! It's just a silly misunderstanding!”

“Where were you last night?” Dakota asked, her tone neither aggressive nor passive, her expression inscrutable as ever.

“I—last night? Why, lady, I was out killing some tramp and stringing her from a crane—what do you want me to say? I was at my uncle's bar until like three AM.”

Dakota scowled now. “Was your uncle at this bar?”

“Hell yeah. Of course. He always stays late. I helped him clean, too.”

Dakota sighed, dropping her head now and massaging the bridge of her nose. “Your uncle can vouch for you? Anyone else?”

“I... hey... hey yeah, wait!” He suddenly exclaimed, beaming. “My uncle can vouch for me! Ha! He saw me there all night! Ahaha! We got cameras inside 'n' everything!" Now Mr. Haines was beaming. He slapped a hand against the table. "There we go! My uncle saw me all night. My aunt lives above the bar; she would've heard me leave."

"Heard you?" Dakota said.

He snorted. "Half the block heard me leave. Like three AM. I drive a Hellcat." He beamed and puffed his scrawny chest a bit at this declaration.

Dakota frowned and turned slowly. "Hellcat?" she said, frowning at Marcus.

He cleared his throat. "A car," he said. "It's loud. Intentionally loud."

"Yeah. It's loud!" Haines repeated as if he'd just played a trump card. "Really loud! My aunt heard it. My uncle saw me. Darn—I have the perfect... what's the word? Abily? Ability?"

"Alibi?" Marcus guessed.

Haines clicked his fingers and pointed, brushing sweaty, greasy hair from his gaze. "That's it. I've got a perfect ally buy."

Dakota didn't speak for a moment, staring across the table. Then, in a clipped tone, she said, "I'm going to need the number for your uncle's bar, and also for your aunt."

"Done!" Haines said, cackling. "So can I go now? I didn't kill no one! Couldn't have cuz of my great..." He looked to Marcus again.

"Alibi."

He pointed.

Dakota sighed, shaking her head, snatching the folder from the table. "You've admitted to running a chop shop. You tried to stab my partner. I think you're going to stay here for a bit longer while we check your... alibi."

She shook her head in disgust, but only once. She didn't allow herself to sulk. Within a span of seconds, she was straight-postured, even-keeled again. She didn't look back, though, as, folder in hand, she pushed out of the interrogation room and stepped into the hall, moving with a bit of a bounce to her step as if she couldn't wait to leave Mr. Haines behind.

Marcus shot the man a look, sighed, then followed hastily after his partner.

CHAPTER EIGHT

Dakota stood in the stairwell of the precinct, one hand clenched, resisting the urge to slam it against the wall. She inhaled shakily, trying to calm herself. The stairwell smelled of mildew and sweat, and the faint murmur of voices drifted from the hall adjacent to the landing above her.

Hinges creaked, and she felt a faint gust of stale air as the door behind her opened and closed again.

She looked over, attentive all at once. Her hand still clenched at her side, and she felt the way her knuckles strained beneath the skin. "So?" she said. "What did you find?"

Marcus crossed his arms, one hand holding his phone. "Alibi checks out. His aunt and uncle confirm, but we also caught that Hellcat of his on a parking lot camera about thirty minutes from the crime scene at the estimated time of death."

"Was he driving?"

Marcus shook his head. "Car was parked. Lights on inside the uncle's bar. We also found a receipt for the drinks he ordered. Timestamped well after two AM."

"Shit," Dakota said, letting out a long puff of air.

Marcus nodded. "Crap."

She turned away for a second, studying the blank wall.

"It was just one suspect, Steele," Marcus insisted. "Don't let it get to you. This is the job. We miss more than we hit. Just gotta keep swinging."

Dakota glanced over. "A baseball metaphor?"

"I mean... Yeah."

"In my sport," she said, "if you miss more than you hit, you lose." She tilted her head back, staring at the ceiling and exhaling a long sigh. She could feel her nerves now. Could feel the desire to second-guess her aptitude. Already, she had Agent Carter breathing down her neck. But more importantly, Dakota needed to decide if coming back had been the right decision after all. What if she'd made a mistake? What if she was going to lead to another—

She unclenched her hand, exhaling sharply through her teeth.

“Dakota,” Marcus said, “maybe we should focus on the first victim?”

She took a second, forcing herself to calm down, to reorient. Then she nodded once. “Alright—what do we know?” She held up a single finger then answered her own question. “A college junior who went missing.”

Marcus held up two fingers. “She was found the next day, her body posed.”

Dakota held up a third. “The scrapyard where she was discovered was nearly twenty miles from the school.”

Both of them lowered their hands, scowling. “This killer,” Marcus said, “clearly has an affinity for junkyards...”

“His weird creations might be a better angle to look at... Why is he twisting their bodies into metal contraptions?”

“Some sort of statement, obviously.”

Dakota hesitated, frowning, and thinking back to the state of the bodies. Both with minimal damage. No evidence of sexual assault. Why was the killer posing them?

“Mind pulling up those crime scene photos?”

Marcus, phone still in hand, obliged, opening the file attached to a nondescript email. The two of them scanned the images. Dakota hid her distaste, frowning at the first victim's pose. As if she'd been flying—wings attached to her back. A tripod, of sorts, soldered to the metal sleeve while holding her aloft.

“Both of them have that in common,” she murmured. “Flight. Or height.”

“Why do you think that is?”

“He's raising them up,” Dakota replied, shaking her head. “Helping them ascend?”

“So we have some sort of psychotic break?” Marcus shook his head. “Hate that.”

“Which part?”

“It's often easier to catch psychopaths. They're predictable. The ones who are truly mentally unwell are harder.”

Dakota didn't disagree. In the former case, motives were often easier to place. But when it came to derangement, it was like trying to locate an appropriate key to fit into a lock. One was never certain until they heard the *click.*

She could tell Marcus was eyeing her now, and she wasn't sure she much liked it. “What?” she said, turning to meet his gaze.

He held his tongue.

"What?" she repeated, louder.

He sighed, glancing about, standing in the privacy of the stairwell. Then he muttered, "Just wondering how you're doing..."

He spoke it with such gentleness and concern Dakota hated how she physically reacted. Her body tensed. She felt a flare of irritation. Not at Marcus, per se, but at the reminder. How was she doing? Suggesting the answer could be one way or another. She didn't like thinking about what Marcus must have gone through when she'd up and left. At the time, she hadn't seen any other choice.

She supposed she owed him something. A question like that from most, and she likely would've dodged or left. But from Marcus?

"Fine," she said. "Fine..."

He didn't reply, allowing the silence to linger, forcing her to give more in response. She sighed. "Really, it's going fine. I'm doing okay, Marcus—I swear. I've been sober since Rapid City, if that's what you're worried about."

"It wasn't. That's not what I was asking at all. I wanted to know how you're doing."

She shrugged. "I don't know what else to say—fine. I need to solve this case. That much is obvious."

Marcus looked away, rubbing ruefully at his chin. "Huh—yeah... I noticed that, too. Agent Carter doesn't seem to... *get* you yet."

"Like," Dakota said. "That word you're looking for is like. Even I can define that one, big guy. She hates my guts. I'm not even sure why. You got any insight?"

Marcus gave a helpless little shake. "I think she was called in to clean up Drafuss's mess. Maybe she sees you as a threat to her regime... I don't know. She treats me well enough, and if you give her time, she grows on you."

Dakota snorted. "Just what I need. Her to be a bigger threat."

"Not that type of growing. Really—she's a good leader, just..."

"Rude? Obnoxious?"

Marcus sighed. "I was going to say blunt. Like you."

Dakota winced. She couldn't think of anything more horrifying than being compared to Agent Carter. She shook her head, glancing back at his phone with the crime scene photos, then looking up at Marcus. "We good on the wellness check?"

He shook his head. "I'm not trying—I'm just worried about you, Steele."

"I get it. But don't be. I'm fine." She patted the big man on the arm and flashed a quick smile. But then, she turned, looking away. "We need more information," Dakota said simply. "You want to drive?"

"Where to?"

"The college campus. I want to speak with the first victim's roommates."

Marcus shrugged, stowing his phone, and stepping aside to let Dakota slip past him, taking the stairs two at a time as she picked up the pace.

For her part, Dakota did her best to keep the second-guessing at bay. All of this used to be so instinctual. She had to get back to that point. When she didn't double-check everything that she thought. It was wasting time. Time they didn't have if the killer kept escalating.

CHAPTER NINE

Sparks buzzed through the air, jumping, and leaping like fairies off the metal, beneath the heat of his tool. The craftsman shifted, adjusting his protective face-shield and analyzing his newest creation from a higher angle.

"There we go," he said in a coaxing, airy voice. He'd often been told he had a girl's voice. More than once teased about it when he was going through puberty. At thirty-three, though, he'd heard it all before. Besides, he quite liked his own voice. It made him... unique.

Every artist's dream.

He reached down and grabbed a cloth, wiping some of the soot stains from the edge of the newest piece. Only a one-sixth scale model of what he intended to do, but he liked to make sure the rehearsal led to a properly executed event. Behind him, from his old record player, he heard the concerto warbling through his studio, the strings and bass and brass all winding their story through the threatened silence.

He frowned, wincing at a faint blemish under the chin of the statuette.

"No, no, no," he said in that high-pitched voice of his. "That's not right. That's not..." he trailed off, glancing over the edge of his workbench towards the plastic container of rejects.

More than fifteen little metal statues—all of them imperfect in one way or another. Still, practice made perfect.

He refocused, picking up a sanding tool and attacking the blemish with gusto. As he did, the sound of the record player behind him came louder as the music reached a crescendo. He paused, closing his eyes, smiling behind his metal mask, and listening.

He'd never been much of a musician himself. He preferred crafting with his hands, but he appreciated all the arts. As the music faded again, he sighed, lowering his little statue, and glancing at the corkboard on the wall.

And there she was.

His Mona Lisa. His muse.

His next project. The first two had gone well enough, but he could feel himself coming into his stride. Could feel himself finding his voice as an artist.

He whistled along with the music in the background as he studied the printed photos of *her.* Nearly twenty photos from different angles, all different sizes.

There she was walking into her place of work. And there was one where she'd dropped something in her living room and was trying to find it beneath the couch. He hadn't taken photos of her in the shower, of course—he had boundaries. He wasn't some creep.

Still, as he stared at her image, those beautiful brown eyes, long lashes, perfectly shaped chin, he couldn't help but shiver. He glanced at his little statute, then up again, then wrinkled his nose. Far from perfect.

He snorted and tossed the rejected creation into the plastic container behind the workbench. The metal *clanked* against the other rejects, and he reached up, lowering his visor and allowing the faint breeze from the desk fan to cool his features.

He had more than pictures, of course. He also had videos of her—at work, at home, on dates. He'd been watching her for a while now.

But... perhaps what this piece needed was a little bit of *soul.* He frowned, considering it, using the cloth from earlier to wipe at his forehead with the clean edge to avoid leaving a streak of ash.

Yes... now was the time. He could feel it.

He had an affinity for gauging the proper timing of this sort of thing. He pulled off his leather work gloves with shaking hands, tossing them onto the scarred worktable. Then, he pulled his phone from his pocket, fingers still trembling.

The music in the background swelled again, and it felt as if it were carrying him forward, ushering him into the unknown.

Every great creator snagged something of the divine and brought it back for mortal eyes. He leaned back in his chair now—a chair he'd had to reinforce for his large frame. His muscles bunched in his back as he tried to find a comfortable position, phone in hand.

He stared at her picture on the wall, eyes hooded. He'd found her the same way he'd found the others. And just like everyone, she needed his help. He paused, staring at the picture, his mind conjuring images of another woman who'd needed his help.

He could remember her screams. Remember the way she'd beaten him, again and again. He could remember his own fall from grace. He snarled, trying not to think of the painful prick followed by the subsequent release of pleasure. He was clean now. He'd purged himself.

But her?

He stared at the images... his muse, for just how broken she was. Beautifully broken. A small, sensitive, delicate thing pleading and begging with her flesh for him to reassemble, readjust, restore.

That's what he did, didn't he?

He made old things new.

He smiled as he considered it all.

And then he called her.

The number he'd managed to swipe from that roster. She also had a number online for work. He kept both saved—equally precious.

He waited, leaning back, allowing the phone to ring.

No answer.

No problem. People were in the habit of ignoring calls from unfamiliar numbers the first time. But on a second call?

He dialed again.

The mind would go wild. *What if this is someone I know? What if it's an opportunity? What if it's some important tax call? What if...*

Then, inevitably, on the second ring—

"Hello?" a pleasant, sunny voice on the other end.

His eyes widened. He perked up in his oversized chair. He leaned forward, resting one hand gently against his wooden table, the other pressing his phone tightly to his ear.

"H-hello?" he said, breathing heavily. Too heavily. He didn't want to come across as some sort of prick. He tried to hold his breath, but this only made things worse, and he ended up gasping into the device. "Hello, Heather?" he said. His voice really was quite high-pitched. He winced, trying to control his excitement.

"Who is this?"

"Your friend," he whispered. "And you..." he let out a little gasp of pleasure.

"Jer? Is that you?" the voice snorted. "This isn't funny; knock it off. We need to talk. Alright? Stop hiding—let's figure this out."

He wrinkled his nose at the pet name she'd given. He hated that name. Hated anything that wasn't his true name. "I just need you to know something," he whispered.

"Jer? Hang on—who is this really?"

"Your savior. And you, dearest, are my muse. I just wanted you to know that before... well... You're my muse."

"I—who is this?" the voice went colder, harsher.

That was what he'd been missing. He glanced towards his pile of rejected sculptures. The face was too soft, too gentle. No—this one, this masterpiece had an edge.

He grinned. "Thank you. You've solved it. I'll see you soon, dear. Very soon."

"Don't call me again. I'm blocking this numb—"

He hung up, letting out another little exhale. He smiled, a dreamy expression on his face as he stared at the photos on his corkboard. Now he knew what he had to do. He had the missing piece.

And soon, very soon, the small one-sixth scale sculpture would give him the reference he needed for the full piece. His muse would play a vital role in both. A central role.

He could barely contain his delight as he stooped and snatched another block of metal from beneath the table, whistling along with the crooning from the record player.

CHAPTER TEN

Dakota sat in the passenger seat, frowning through the windshield as her partner drove them through the Chicago suburbs in the afternoon sunlight; they sped away from the city towards the small college town where there seemed to be a church on every street.

In the distance, along a road lined with restaurants and fast-food joints and auto repair centers, she spotted a large, sandstone protrusion.

"Ah," Marcus said, noticing the same landmark. "I believe that's the school's belfry."

Dakota gave a little snort of air. A belfry at a school? She shook her head in amazement. Her high school had taken place in a three-room building that had once been a failed supermarket. After losing her way, getting back on track, finishing her GED, and heading off to college, she'd been older than most of the other students and had lived off campus. Half her courses had been over the internet.

"A belfry," she murmured, frowning.

She was still mulling over the two crime scenes, attempting to make sense of them. The strange way the killer had used metal while posing the bodies. The care he'd taken not to injure the skin. But why these two women specifically? They had no connection. One was educated, upper-class. The other a high-school dropout. Homeless.

"Both victims were vulnerable targets," Dakota murmured. "What if that's as simple as it gets. He's simply targeting the vulnerable. Crimes of opportunity."

Marcus hit his blinker, turning down a side-street as he moved closer to the college. "The victims were opportunistic but..."

"But the crime scenes weren't," Dakota said quickly before he could. A second later, she realized she'd cut her partner off. "Sorry," she said. "Just..."

"No, you're right. The crime scenes were meticulously planned. Odds of him just choosing a random stranger as the centerpiece of his creations..."

"Low," Dakota said, nodding. "Very low. Flabbergasting." She cocked an eyebrow. "Wasn't that one of your words? This case is flabbergasting."

Marcus snorted, but then resumed a more professional expression as he pulled into the driveway of a large, two-story suburban home. "This is it," he said, nodding towards the house. "She lived off campus."

Dakota quickly took in what she could of their surroundings. Three cars parked in the two-car driveway. The garage door was closed. Lights illuminated the street from the house. Her gaze skipped to the glass door. She spotted a few pairs of shoes stacked neatly by a welcome mat inside the porch. The shoes were all about the same size, none small enough to belong to a child.

A college house indeed.

She pushed out of the car and approached the front door. Two curt knocks then a quick, polite ringing of the doorbell.

Dakota shifted uncomfortably on the stairs, and it took her a moment to realize why. Girls like these, wealthy, educated girls, had often been her nemesis when she'd been younger. Perhaps that was why Agent Carter disliked her—maybe it was something Dakota was giving off.

She forced a smile, standing there, but then felt this was dishonest and let her lips curve back into a neutral expression.

A second later, the door swung open.

Marcus was standing a few steps back. A trick he'd picked up after the first few years of working with Dakota. He was such a large, intimidating figure; often by stepping a few paces back, it made him appear smaller through keyholes.

Like this, with Dakota in the doorway, Marcus a few paces away, they were confronted by a yawning, blonde woman with a round face.

She stood in the doorway, glancing between the two of them. "Umm, hi?" she said carefully. Dakota noted the way she kept one foot braced against the bottom of the door.

"FBI," Dakota said. "I'm Agent Steele. This is Agent Clement. We're here to speak with you about your roommate, Caitlynn Jackson."

The girl let out a little sigh, blinking a few times as if she'd just woken from a nap. "Again?" she said. She sucked air, but then repeated the word, trying to smooth over the impatient tone in the first attempt. "Again, oh. Alright then. Is it okay if we speak out here?" She shot a look over her shoulder. "My roommate's boyfriend is in from out of town, and they haven't seen each other for like, you know, *months.*"

Dakota stepped back, making space. The girl turned on a light, stepped onto the porch and closed the door shut behind her, leaving only a crack. She turned back to the two agents, forcing a quick smile and a shrug. “So how can I help? They've already taken our report. Public safety has been by twice.”

“Public who?”

“College security,” Marcus murmured.

The girl tapped her nose and pointed at him.

“How about we start with names,” Dakota said.

“Oh, yes. I'm Claire. You said you're Steele. And you're Clement. Did I get that right? *Clement.*”

“Perfect,” Marcus said. He'd stepped onto the porch now but remained behind Dakota.

Dakota, though, wasn't about to go through this a second time. In the past, Marcus had always been the one to do the talking. She preferred watching, listening and scrutinizing. She shuffled to the side now and allowed the big man center stage.

“Well, Claire,” Marcus said in that congenial way of his, “we don't intend to take much of your time. But I'm sure you know a lot of people are working on Caitlynn's case.”

Claire bit her lip and nodded once. “It was so terrible,” she said in a small voice. “But I just don't know how to help. None of us were with her when... when it happened.”

“We understand that. We were wondering if you knew anyone who might have wanted to hurt your roommate.”

Another sigh, a quick scratch behind an ear and a tug on golden bangs. “No. Nothing like that. People liked Caitlynn. She was a private person, but most of us are.”

“No ex-boyfriend? No angered lover? No stalker?”

“Nothing like that. I—I told all this to the police.”

Dakota cleared her throat. “What makes you say Caitlynn was a private person?”

Claire's eyes bounced from Marcus to Dakota now. “I—well, I mean it's just sort of a vibe, you know.”

“Can you think of anything specific?”

Claire hesitated. “I mean... she never mentioned if she was dating anyone. She didn't talk too much about her dad, but I think that's just because he's rich. Or was... I mean, he is still rich. But he's not still—well maybe...” Claire trailed off, pausing to compose herself.

“Did you sense that she was trying to hide who she was dating?”

Claire smirked, but quickly hid the expression. “Umm—no. I sensed that she wasn't dating anyone but didn't want us to know.”

Dakota glanced at Marcus, then back towards the young woman. "Is there anything else you can think of?"

"Umm... Not really. I mean," she paused, shrugging one shoulder. "There was Wednesday nights. But I mentioned that to the police also."

Dakota perked. "What about Wednesday nights?"

"It probably isn't anything, but she'd leave campus every Wednesday, then walk home. Like late."

"She walked home late at night?"

"Yeah... I mean, she wasn't—you know—killed Wednesday. So I didn't think—"

"What was she doing?"

"Like I said, she was a private person. She refused to get a ride from *anyone.* I offered like three times and nearly got my head bit off for it. I never asked again."

Dakota hesitated, considering these words. Why would a college-aged woman refuse a ride late at night? Embarrassment? For the exercise? Dakota frowned. "You don't have any clue why she was gone on Wednesdays?"

Claire rubbed at her arm, wincing and half glancing back at the door. "Like I said, she never wanted to talk about it."

"But you never speculated? Never talked among the other roommates?"

Claire sighed. "I mean... Look, *I* didn't know anything. But Steff seemed to think she'd figured it out. We called it the Mystery of Wednesday." Claire smiled, but then winced and hid it again. "Steff said she heard rattling in their shared bathroom."

"Rattling?"

"Yeah—but like, you know... *rattling.*"

Dakota just stared blankly.

"Pills," Marcus said.

Dakota blinked. "Oh. So you think your roommate had a pill problem?"

"I don't. Steff did. Besides what does it matter anyway? Caitlynn is dead. You don't think..." She paused, biting her lip, and looking embarrassed suddenly. She shook her head, glancing off, but then mustered the courage and finished, "Are *we* in danger? This guy isn't like... you know... going to come back, is he?"

In that moment, Dakota glimpsed a crack in the facade. Tired, bored, weary from studying though she was, the young woman was also scared. Very scared.

Dakota wished she had something to say to comfort the woman. Part of her almost envied a life so accustomed to living *without* fear. Most of Dakota's life growing up had been moving from one tragedy to the next. Fear had been part of her, had shaped and molded her in the oddest ways.

Girls like this had often been the ones to... Dakota blinked, realizing the train of thought. A niggling part of her didn't *know* how to comfort someone like this. In the end, she just exhaled faintly and then tried her best. Marcus was the one who handled emotions, but Dakota felt it would've been inappropriate to look to him.

Instead, she said, "You're going to be fine." She looked the girl in the eyes, forcing a quick smile but then letting it die on her lips. She nodded. "You're safe. We'll have units patrolling the campus. Your college has doubled security for the next few months."

The girl swallowed at this, but Dakota could see a visible sag in her shoulders as if a weight had been lifted. But then she tensed again. "You—you'll find the killer? The guy who did this?"

Dakota didn't like making a habit of dishonesty. She hated saying things she knew were untrue.

But after only a moment of hesitation, she nodded firmly. "We will. I promise."

The girl sighed, but then just as quickly covered by shrugging and shaking her head. She even added an attempt at a yawn. "I mean, no big deal. I'm not worried. Look, I really have to get back to studying. Is that all?"

Dakota considered this for a moment. But there was still another thought she hadn't rounded out. "One final thing, what do you think pills had to do with Wednesday?"

"That's obvious, isn't it?"

Dakota sighed and gave another blank look.

Claire leaned in, whispering, "She was obviously meeting her dealer. She didn't want a ride because she didn't want anyone knowing. Now, please—can I go?"

Marcus nodded warmly. "Thank you very much, Claire. We appreciate your time."

The girl gave a little, limp-wristed wave and pushed back into the house, shutting the door behind her. A pause, then there came a click of a lock. From where Dakota stood, the locking mechanism on this side of the door looked brand-new.

She didn't blame them for taking precautions.

Dakota frowned at the door. Marcus was scratching at his chin, but when she looked, it seemed like he was trying to hide a smile.

"What?" she demanded.

He shook his head. "Nothing."

"Oh come on—what are you giggling at?"

He sobered up, but still smiled warmly. "I'm just happy to see you back. I've always known how kind you are—it's nice when others get to see it too." He looked like he wanted to add more. He paused, glancing towards the new lock on the door. Instead of addressing her, though, he just nodded towards the mechanism. "Would be hard to get through that, wouldn't it?"

She stared then shrugged. "It's a locked door, Clement. Yeah. It'd be hard." She began to consider if perhaps there was another meaning behind her partner's words, but before she could think on it, her phone suddenly began to ring. Marcus's followed a second later.

Dakota glanced back at the big man, feeling her stomach twist as she pulled the device from her pocket. "Hello?" she said.

"Agent Steele?" said an unfamiliar voice. "This is Captain Hubbard. We need you to meet us at the Midwest Hauling Yard."

Dakota felt her skin prickle. "Another body?" she said. She didn't need the response to know the truth. Her stomach fell out the bottom of her feet. Her jaw clenched.

"Yeah," the cop replied. "Another body."

Dakota was already moving down the stairs again, hastening towards their car.

CHAPTER ELEVEN

Dakota could feel a strange gravity over Chicago's finest as she stepped into the victim's house.

Behind her, she left the scene of flashing blue and red lights, barking voices, and the sound of stomping footsteps. The house itself was massive. An expensive, luxurious mansion just bordering the city. Also, it had been fifteen minutes from the college.

Dakota wrinkled her nose, turning to look over her shoulder in the direction of the junkyard just visible past the first row of trees. This particular subdivision was new. The house itself was brand-new. The trees lining the pavements were young and spry. The junkyard, still visible, despite landscapers' best efforts, would eventually be replaced by the expanding subdivision of luxury homes.

But now, a far more ominous scene tugged at her attention.

Dakota turned to look at the body.

And this was where she found the source of the strange aura, the quiet murmurs, the uncomfortable glances.

The victim, according to Marcus, had been a high-powered attorney who had worked with survivors of domestic abuse. Now, she stood on a coffee table, her arms stretched on either side of her, her legs wrapped in molten steel.

Her arms were suspended by two metal brackets along her elbows and attached to her shoulders.

Dakota shivered as she stared at the bizarre spectacle. Lights flashed as crime scene photographers did their work. Marcus Clement was already speaking to one of the first responders, their voices low and muted from the adjacent kitchen.

Dakota couldn't help but notice the thick, metal door. The windows had steel bars. Clearly, a lawyer who worked with abuse victims had to take precautions.

But why had the precautions not kept her safe?

On a hunch, Dakota began checking the windows, turning her back to the victim for the moment. She moved down the hallway, sidestepping a photographer, and approached the bathroom. She peered into a bedroom and then turned to look through the bathroom.

An empty sink. A lonely toothbrush in a glass cup... The toilet seat was closed. The bathroom mat looked dry...

Then she spotted it. Over the bath—the window. Slightly open, and there, just beyond the edge of the frame: two missing bars on this window.

She hastened forward, stepping into the bathtub, which she noted was dry, to peer at the bars. Melted. Bent like wax.

She gritted her teeth. The killer had known how to get in. He had planned this.

He had known the victim would be home. Alone. He had even chosen a location next to a scrap yard. There went the theory that the victims were random. No. The killer chose them. But he didn't just choose them, he kept an eye on them. There was no way he could've scheduled everything so perfectly if he didn't know Ms. Kramer's schedule. These weren't crimes of opportunity. These were meticulously planned. Down to the last detail.

Dakota gritted her teeth, and turned towards the bathroom door.

"Hey, you!" she called, waving a hand.

The photographer she'd passed in the hall ducked his head inside. "Me?"

"Photograph the window. Also, get someone in here to check for prints."

Not that she expected to find any. The photographer nodded quickly and hurried off to grab someone from forensics.

Dakota turned back down the hall, moving once more towards the living room and the horrible scene; again, she was struck by the lack of blood or damage to the victim's skin. Terin Kramer almost looked as if she were sleeping, if not for the cut across her neck.

"Where was she killed?" Dakota called out.

Marcus turned from his conversation and glanced at the woman's neck, then at the table. "They found blood upstairs," he said.

Dakota tried to focus.

"What do you make of it?"

Marcus nodded apologetically to the cop he was speaking with and approached Dakota, studying the body. "More of the same, I guess. The only person this makes sense to is the one we're trying to find."

Dakota grunted.

Marcus said, "All the bodies have been elevated. See that?" He pointed to the coffee table. "Why put her on it. Why use the crane? Why make Caitlynn fly?"

Dakota shook her head. "It's almost like he's trying to honor them..." She winced. That wasn't it. It didn't sound right. But he was treating the corpses with a type of reverence. Posing them like one might an ancient Pharaoh. And what was with the metal work?

"Coroner says the initial findings look accurate. Killed by a single cut across the throat. She bled out on her bed, and then he took her down here.

"Any DNA evidence yet? Any sign of a struggle?"

"Too soon for DNA. No sign of a struggle. Did you find out how he got in here?"

Dakota nodded. "Bathroom. Two bars bent."

Marcus rubbed at the back of his neck. He adjusted his spectacles and gave a quick shake of his head. "Our guy is a professional. All these tools he uses to work the metal—they don't come cheap."

Dakota didn't reply. She'd reached the same conclusion. "Is there a Mr. Kramer?"

Marcus shook his head. "Not here. Upstairs, there's blood by the side of the bed, but the other side hasn't been slept in."

"Separate rooms?"

"No car in the driveway. No male shoes by the door. Plus the toilet seats were all lowered."

Dakota chuckled humorlessly, a single barking sound. "So you're saying he doesn't live here?"

"Affirmative. Why are you so sure there's a husband?"

Dakota pointed at the wall by a bookcase. A few framed photos displayed a woman and a man. The woman was easy to recognize where she stood in the middle of the room. The man, though, was leaning against her, beaming out in the photographs.

"Interesting," Marcus said. "She's married. But he's not here. Think the killer knew that?"

Dakota sighed. "I'm beginning to think the killer knows everything about his victims. Where is the husband, do you think?"

Marcus shook his head. He glanced at his watch. "It's getting late, Dakota."

"I know, I know. I just... I have a hunch."

"A hunch?"

Dakota didn't know what to say. It *was* getting late. The constant driving about the city, the time at the crime scene, speaking with the police and speaking with the roommates had bled into night quickly enough. But she didn't want to sleep. Couldn't even fathom the idea of resting her head on a hotel pillow. She hated hotels. But mostly she hated unsolved cases. Besides, in the past, hotels had been a vector for ruining sobriety. Almost two weeks sober, and she didn't want to break the streak. Not just to impress the new boss, not just to solve the case, but because in a way, finding these killers was a rush. The closest she could think of was stepping into a cage for a fight. She could remember the bright lights, the crowd screaming. Could remember her coach shouting instructions from the corner that were mostly left unheeded because she couldn't hear them.

Eventually, it all came down to two fighters and a referee. The door would close behind her, with a loud *clang,* she would face her opponent, and only one of them would emerge as victor.

The adrenaline came long before she stepped into the ring, but it rarely subsided until she was done.

In a way, drinking had always been the worst when she didn't have fights.

Catching killers brought that same rush, that same surge of adrenaline, of meaning...

No, she wasn't ready to go to bed. She wasn't ready to try to explain any of it to Marcus either.

She turned, giving a little flick of her hand. "I'll be quick; I just want to speak with some of the neighbors."

"It's late, Steele!" he called.

"It's fine," she countered.

Marcus jogged to keep up with her. "What are you going to ask the neighbors?"

"These are all fancy, expensive houses. Places like this always have cameras. I'm just going to see if anyone saw anything." Dakota shrugged, patted Marcus on the arm, and then pushed back out the door, grateful to leave the grisly spectacle behind her.

She glanced up and down the street, looking for a good candidate, chose a particularly large, red brick home, and made a beeline towards it, marching up the street.

CHAPTER TWELVE

The dark skies quickly intruded across the horizon. Night fell around Dakota, bringing with it a chill breeze. The small, newly planted saplings lining the fresh sidewalks shuddered and shivered in the wind, providing little protection against the elements.

Dakota rubbed her arms as she picked up the pace, glancing through metal gates or over low-lying walls. The houses here were all larger than any she'd seen back home. Off to the left, she could still see the junkyard, slowly losing ground to the expanding subdivision.

She exhaled faintly as she peered through a gate towards a large home. It had a small sign warning about a security system, but no visible door cam. She moved down the sidewalk, picking up the pace. Marcus was still back in the victim's house, crossing T's and dotting I's. Eventually, he'd come looking for her.

But Dakota wasn't ready to go to their hotel.

Not yet. Not with so few leads.

She passed the metal fence and faced another home, this one with a sleek Mercedes in the driveway. A faint flicker of light, then the shimmer of reflective glass caught her eye.

She paused, staring over the low, brick wall. The house had a white turret with a small blue flag on top... She wasn't sure what to make of the décor. But what *did* catch her attention was the door cam facing the street.

She felt a flicker of excitement and pushed through the gate, hastening up the cobblestone sidewalk to the front door of the mansion. She rang the doorbell and waited. The sound from inside the house echoed and chirped like a twittering bird. Even rich people's doorbells sounded different.

She waited patiently, then tried again.

A light went on inside. She heard muffled voices, then the sound of rapid footsteps.

"FBI!" she called, knocking in three short, staccato bursts.

More faint muttering. Something that sounded like, "...lawyer..." Then shadows appeared on the other side of the opaque, stained glass entry door.

Were they talking about the lawyer who'd been killed, or wondering if they ought to get a lawyer of their own?

"Hello?" a timid voice probed out into the night. The door remained shut.

"Hello," Dakota replied. "My name is Agent Dakota Steele. I'm afraid there's been an incident in your neighborhood. I'm looking for witness testimony. Do you have a moment?"

"Umm... Not right now. It's late!"

Dakota paused, then tried again. "I need to speak to you, please. It's about a murder. Time is of the essence."

The word *murder* seemed to do it. The door flung open.

Two figures huddled together in the doorway, both looking like carbon copies of the other though one was a man, the other a woman. The man had a bit of a belly pushing against silk pajamas. So did his wife. The woman had hair curlers and wore a sleeping mask. Her husband didn't have the curlers, but a slick green paste covered his skin. They were both about five foot even and both had small hands which were twitching against each other.

The man blinked from behind the green gunk. "What happened?" he said. "We've been watching the police cars come and go for about an hour. Would've kept watching if not for work."

"In the morning," his wife replied. She patted her husband proudly on the back. "He's a banker."

"I'm a banker," he said.

Dakota blinked. "Right. Well, I actually was wondering if I could get a look at the footage on your door cam..." she trailed off hopefully.

The man frowned. "We have a door cam?"

His wife said, "Got it last month, remember Arnold? Because of those sign-stealers."

"Oh, yes. Wait—but what's a door cam?"

The woman sighed. "A camera on our door, Arnold."

"Right, right," he said, nodding quickly. A fleck of green splatted the ground.

Dakota massaged the bridge of her nose but tried to pass it off as a scratch. "I won't need it long. Just the footage of tonight."

"What happened?" the power couple said, staring at her, wide-eyed.

"Your neighbor, Mrs. Kramer, was killed." Normally, it was frowned on to share details of an ongoing investigation with civilians. But it was late, and Dakota wanted that footage. She didn't have time to dodge the twenty questions that would've followed a non-answer.

The woman gasped. “Mrs. Kramer was *killed*? Dear God, did you hear her Arnold?”

“I heard. I heard. How awful. Of course you can see the footage. Umm—where is the footage, dear?”

“On your tablet, honey.”

“I have a tablet? What's a tablet?”

The woman sighed and held up a finger. “One moment,” she said. She turned and moved back down a hallway, her footsteps quickening.

Dakota watched her leave, tapping her foot against the cobblestone path.

“I liked the Kramers,” the husband said, shaking his head sadly. “Me and Jerry go golfing together sometimes.”

Dakota glanced over. “The victim's husband?”

“Yes, yes. Jerry Kramer. He's a good guy. Pity about their troubles...” he sighed. “Though I guess neither of them saw *this* coming.”

Dakota frowned. “What troubles?”

“Hmm? Did I say troubles. Oh—well, just a marriage spat. You know.”

“Here's the video from tonight!” called a voice from down the hall. A second later, the wife emerged, hefting a small tablet and turning it so Dakota could see it.

But Dakota was distracted now. “Hang on,” she said. “The Kramers were having marital conflict? We noticed Jerry wasn't at the house tonight.”

The couple shared a long look. “He wouldn't be, would he,” said the banker. “No, no. Jerry's been in the city this last week. Staying at a hotel.” He sighed sadly.

“Why is he staying at a hotel? Is that normal for him?”

“No—I wouldn't say *normal.* Just, like I was saying—not that it's any of my business—but the marital problems... It got loud a couple of nights last week.”

Dakota frowned, glancing towards the extended device with the door cam footage. Before she reached out to take it, though, she said, “So he hasn't been home this last week at all? No one would've seen him?”

“Seen him? No—haven't seen him for a week.”

Dakota grunted, taking the iPad and tapping the play button. The video image showed the street outside the mansion, but also displayed the front of Mrs. Kramer's home. Dakota rewound and then sped up the playback, scrutinizing the image. She paused it suddenly, staring. “Whose car is that?” she said, tapping the video.

“Umm, mine,” the man said. “Just got in from work there.”

Dakota nodded and continued watching as the car pulled past Mrs. Kramer's house. She watched as evening turned to night. No sign of the killer. No sign of anyone sneaking up on the house across the street. Dakota realized, suddenly, that the killer had chosen the one window on the first floor that the door cam wouldn't have spotted.

Not only was he meticulous in his preparation, but he was clever. He'd known the camera was there. No cars on the video either. No strangers. No errant, late-night walkers. The killer was one step ahead...

Or... perhaps it was someone who knew the house and knew the neighborhood.

Dakota looked up. “You didn't mention what the cause of their marital troubles were about. Did Mr. Kramer ever mention it?”

“Oh—well I—”

“You said you were golf buddies, didn't you? It never came up?”

The small banker shifted uncomfortably. “It's not really my place to tell tales, but... well, seeing as she's... dead...” He swallowed and flinched. “I guess it can't hurt. I don't judge, mind you. I'm not the judging sort but I heard from Jerry that his wife had a bit of a problem before they were wed...”

“A problem?”

“Umm—she was... how do you say it nicely. A bit of a sex addict. That's what she called it.” He held up his hands as if holding off a mugger. “I don't use the term myself. But she called herself that. They got married anyway—things were going fine. But according to Jerry, he thought his wife was having a relapse. Back into her, er, well, old addiction.”

“So Mr. Kramer thought Mrs. Kramer was cheating on him?”

“You could say that.”

“With who?”

“I don't have a clue. Really, neither did Jerry. He was just... I guess realizing he'd bitten off a bit more than he could chew with this lifestyle. Big house, fancy wife—you know. He definitely married up.”

“How do you mean? Married *up*?”

“Yeah—I mean, Mrs. Kramer was a big shot. Lawyer type. Jerry was a local. He married up.”

Dakota's eyes narrowed. “And what does Mr. Kramer do for a living?”

"Oh—I think he's a fabricator. That's a type of—"

"Welder," Dakota said. "A metalworker."

"Mhmm. That's right. Works in a small shop called *Kramer and Co*. Say, think I could get that back?"

Dakota glanced at the iPad, nodding once. The camera image showed nothing she could use. But this information? Mr. Kramer thought his wife was cheating on him. How that tied in with the other two victims wasn't clear. Maybe he'd been trying to hide his tracks. Or maybe he'd suffered a break. But who else would've known to avoid the cameras, to use the back, bathroom window? Hell, he'd even known when Mrs. Kramer would be home. On top of that—he was a welder.

It fit. It fit *perfectly.*

Of course, that didn't mean he was guilty. It just meant he had means, motive, and opportunity. Plus, according to this neighbor, Jerry had been living in a hotel for a week. No one to keep an eye on his comings and goings. The murders had all taken place while Jerry had been away from the house.

A coincidence?

Or something worth investigating?

Dakota nodded her thanks as she turned. The door shut slowly behind her as she moved back across the street without a farewell. Once they'd decided she was done with them, the door clicked, and she heard a rush of murmuring from inside the house.

The chill in the air nipped at her skin as she picked up her pace and hastened across the street, pulling her phone from her pocket and hastily dialing her partner's number. The phone rang once, twice. She frowned.

"Come on, Clement. Answer..."

But he never did. Instead, Marcus's deep voice echoed from the front seat of their sedan. "Trying to reach me?"

She jolted, turning sharply towards their parked vehicle. The front window was rolled down and Marcus was watching her, his eyebrows raised.

"Let me guess," he said, "You *still* don't want to go get some sleep..." He closed his eyes, shaking his head as he completed a long yawn.

"I'm tired too," Dakota said, but she didn't really mean it. "But I think I have something."

Marcus groaned. "Steele you *promised.* Just the neighbors, *then* sleep."

“No, I know, but I've got something.”

“The door cam check out?”

“No, not that. Mrs. Kramer's husband is a metalworker. They've been having marital issues and he's been MIA for a week.”

Marcus frowned through the window. “Wait, what?”

She shrugged. “Like I said—I think I have something.”

“Do we know where he is right now?”

Dakota shook her head. “The neighbor says he's at a hotel in the city. It might take some time to track him down. But I know where he works—neighbor says he runs a small shop called *Kramer and Co.”*

Marcus grunted, glanced at his phone, typed in the name, then muttered, “It's like twenty minutes away, Dakota...” He sighed, “But... it does look pretty bad for Mr. Kramer.” He sighed again, “Fine—we can check out his shop and get someone back at headquarters to trace credit cards to see if we can find what hotel he's at.”

“Perfect. You can drive.”

“Big whoop. I'm choosing the radio station this time.”

CHAPTER THIRTEEN

Dakota matched Marcus halfway through his own yawn, holding a hand to her lips as they pulled along the curb in a run-down part of the city.

She could feel her eyelids weigh heavy, her limbs and motions lethargic. Maybe Marcus had been right. But even tired, yawning, she could feel her anticipation rising. It started as a prickle along the back of her neck but spread down her arms to the tips of her fingers.

She pushed out of the door, onto the sidewalk in the rundown portion of the neighborhood.

Kramer and Co was a single story, squat cement building that looked like it might have once been an auto shop. The garage doors were locked with padlocks, though, and painted over to blend into the walls. In the dark, Dakota couldn't quite make out the color of the building. Greenish, or maybe light brown.

Marcus clicked the locks to the car, prompting the headlights to flash orange, reflecting off the greasy windows of the shop. There were no lights on inside.

Dakota jammed her hands into her pockets and shot a look at her partner. "Just a quick look around and see if we spot anything."

Marcus nodded, glancing towards the building, a nervous look in his eyes. The big man didn't like investigating in the dark. Most things couldn't scare Marcus Clement, but she had it on good authority that he slept with a nightlight.

"We can't enter the shop without a warrant," Marcus reminded her.

"I know," she said, testily. "But if you see any sculptures in progress, or unconscious women, give me a shout."

Marcus sighed but nodded. He began to move around the right side of the building, peering through the glass windows.

Dakota knew he wanted to get it over with quickly, so to save time, she headed around the other side, brushing against the green painted garage doors.

She detected the scent of kerosene and something sweet. The ground looked like it had been recently cleaned with a power washer.

She frowned. Maintenance? Or removing stains?

Her eyes moved to the garage doors, glancing at the faintest gap between the cement and the metal. She wondered what Jerry Kramer kept inside the shop so late at night. Besides, where had he been staying these last seven days? Was it really just a coincidence that women, including his wife, started to die at the hands of a metalworker the same week that he disappeared from his house?

Dakota moved cautiously, slipping around the side of the building and hastening down a dark alley created by the shop and an old office complex.

The walls were bare. The alley itself was narrow, and it took her a second to spot the small window about twelve feet in the air at the very top of the structure. She frowned. How was she going to look through that?

She glanced about, her eyes landing on the low wall pressed against the office. If she used the wall to reach the window frame on the second floor of the complex, she might be able to peer through the garage window.

She glanced back over her shoulder. "Marcus?" she called.

A pause. Then a hushed response, "Everything alright?"

"Do you see anything?"

Another pause. Then the sound of fingers tapping against glass. "Not much. Nothing suspicious. What about you?"

Dakota felt her stomach twist. Part of her wanted Marcus to shout that he'd seen a body or a man standing with a bloody dagger. She wasn't willing to go back without a clue which meant she had to look in that twelve-foot window. "Not yet!" she called.

She heard a faint murmur, then the sound of footsteps moving further away as Marcus slunk around the building's other side.

Dakota let out a long breath. No point in hesitating; she'd come here for a reason and wasn't about to back out because of a small obstacle.

She gripped the dusty wall. The grainy surface pressed against her fingers, causing prickles along her back. She dusted her hand off, and tried again, pushing easily onto the concrete surface. She hadn't been a fighter in a while, but she still worked out as if she was one. Now, perched on the wall, she reached the metal bars over the window to the office complex. Gripping these, and testing them, she began to pull herself up the window. Rust trickled from a gap between the bars in the wall. She winced, staring at this weak point. But three other bars held in place. She reached the top of the window, standing twelve feet in the air now. She took a moment to catch her breath, exhaling slowly and standing in the dark, wedged between the two buildings.

Now came the hard part. She had to turn around and peer into the garage.

She moved slowly, meticulously, rotating at the hips and wincing as she did. And then, once she was settled, she leaned forward, her hands behind her back, gripping the metal bars, her feet braced against the sill, and her eyes fixated on the window.

Dusty, but big enough to give her an angle onto the workshop's floor.

She winced, unable to make out much in the dark. There was a large shape, which she took for some type of machine. Or was it a car?

She leaned a bit further, her body angling over the alley floor. She tried not to imagine how painful it would be if the bar behind her broke and she was sent tumbling.

She eased back a bit just in case.

More rust trickled behind her. Through the windows, she did her best to make out anything in the dark. A shadow flickered, and she stared, but a second later she realized it was a standing fan, moving slowly to cast a breeze about the room.

She swallowed, her lips very dry all of a sudden. She winced, readjusting her grip on the wall, careful to secure her perch.

In the distance, she heard voices—laughter. The sound of a smashing bottle, then the sounds faded. She released a puff of air, trying to focus. But it was just so difficult to make anything out in the dark.

She thought she spotted a blinking red light inside the shop. A camera? Or a computer charger?

She hissed sharply beneath her breath. This wouldn't do. She needed access to the place. Marcus liked to play by the rules. In fact, she was pretty sure Marcus invented half the rules.

But she was trying to get a job done—maybe a busted window was in order.

No, no—Agent Carter would have her ass. Dakota cursed, shaking her head in frustration. There was no way for her to see what was inside the shop from this angle.

For a moment, she considered calling out for Marcus again. But then, she heard a sudden *crunch.*

She turned sharply, and at the same time heard a voice from the exit to the alley.

"Put your hands where I can see them! Don't move."

She stared as a figure emerged in the alley. A figure holding a gun pointed directly at her. She froze, her fingers going cold where they gripped her precarious hold. “Hang on!” she called down. She stared wide-eyed at the gun-wielding figure. He stalked up the alley, his eyes blazing, his teeth set. She glanced sharply past him. No sign of Marcus.

She was on her own.

“I said put your hands up!” He waved the gun at her face. Dakota tried to move, but if she lifted her hands, she was going to fall. The man, twitchy as he was, would undoubtedly see any motion—even accidental—as a threat.

Crap. Now she wished she'd taken Marcus's advice. Wished she'd just gone to bed.

CHAPTER FOURTEEN

Dakota nearly fell as she tried to navigate her position. Thankfully, she managed to retain her grip. The man emerging at the exit to the alley kept the weapon pointed as he drew nearer. He stepped forward, the streetlights illuminating his face.

A very handsome man. A strange thing to notice with a gun pointed at her, but this was testament to just how good looking the person was.

He had puppy dog eyes, long eyelashes, and a sculpted jawline—not too sharp, which might have made him look like a Neanderthal, and not too underdeveloped. He had faint stubble, a nose like Henry Cavill, and cheekbones that belonged in an autumn catalog.

The handsome man, though, was scowling at her.

"Who are you?" he demanded.

Dakota said, carefully, "Listen closely, my name is Dakota Steele. I'm an agent with the FBI. Please lower the gun."

The man snorted. "Nice try. Keep your hands where I can see them."

Dakota winced. "I'm not sure if you've noticed, but if I let go of this bar, I'm going to fall."

The man was shifting uncomfortably now, bouncing from one foot to the other, his face flushed. Even with the redness creeping into his cheeks, he was still beautiful.

Dakota tried to force herself to focus. "I'm going to get down, slowly. Don't shoot me. My identification is in my pocket."

"Don't move!" he snapped, his voice shrill. "I'm warning you. Keep your hands up."

Now, Dakota was growing frustrated. She didn't believe that good looks and good brains couldn't exist in the same body, but this man was threatening to reinforce the stereotype.

"Look, I'm gonna move very slowly," she said. "Very, *very* slowly." As she said it, she lowered herself. She winced, trying not to imagine a bullet through the spine as she dropped. She was forced to turn, to navigate the window then drop onto the wall.

The man with the gun was still breathing heavily but at least for the moment he wasn't ventilating her.

Once she sat on the wall, she put her hands in the air. She slipped off the edge of the wall and landed nimbly on her feet, dust falling behind her. She faced the man with the weapon. "Are you Jerry Kramer?"

His expression flashed with panic. "Who's asking?"

"I told you. My name is Agent Steele."

He gestured with the gun. "Hands up."

She put her hands higher.

By his reaction, she guessed she had him pegged.

She didn't like having a gun pointed at her head, but she also could tell, even from here, that the safety was on. This wasn't necessarily a good thing. Amateur shooters could be just as dangerous as professional ones. You could never tell what they were going to do. For the moment, though, she remained calm. She didn't want to direct his attention towards the safety. As long as he didn't realize he wouldn't be able to shoot, she was fine. Besides, this was an opportunity.

Back in her fighting days, Dakota had often used a bluff known at her gym as *possum.* Something Coach Little had cooked up on her behalf. Sometimes, especially as a woman in her field, playing possum would invite lines of questioning that wouldn't otherwise be available. In this moment, the man thought he had the advantage. In a way, he did. He had a gun pointed at her. He didn't know about Marcus. And Dakota had her hands in the air.

Sometimes, though, when playing possum, it allowed a fighter in the cage to gather valuable information.

The man didn't know why she was here. Didn't know that he was under investigation. Didn't know if she had seen anything in his shop, whether there was something there or not.

Sometimes, the best way to gain valuable intelligence was to allow the opponent to think they had the upper hand.

With a gun in her face, it wasn't difficult to do.

She kept calm, and said, "I can show you my ID if you like." She began to lower her hand, but he yelled, "Don't move!"

She froze. "Fine. I won't. I'm sorry. You are Mr. Kramer, though, aren't you?"

His teeth pressed together, only further serving to emphasize his jaw and cheekbones. He shook his head furiously. "So what? I'm calling the police."

With one hand he kept the gun pointed at her, and with the other he reached hastily for his pocket. The man's trigger discipline was awful.

The safety was still on, and he wasn't really even aiming at her.

She sighed, though, keeping her hands up. "You've been gone from home for a few days, Mr. Kramer," she said, slowly.

He looked up sharply. He was still holding his phone. "How do you know that?"

"I told you. I'm FBI."

"Yeah right. You're a copper thief. I told you guys the last time, if I caught any of you stealing from my shop again, I'd take care of business myself."

He waved the gun emphatically. Dakota just nodded. "I understand your concern. You're making a mistake, sir." She remained calm. This had always been something she was good at in life-or-death situations, especially when violence was involved. She was content to remain motionless by the wall. For the moment, she didn't sense an immediate threat. And she still wanted information. "Why haven't you been home?"

He snorted, "None of your business."

"I heard your wife had a sex addiction."

She said it carefully, planting the words intentionally. The addiction would be a private matter. Offensive. Using his wife in the past tense, though, was a fishing expedition. She wasn't sure what he would bite on.

He just shook his head. "My wife is a woman—you gals are all the same. Besides, how do you know about that?"

Dakota frowned. Present tense. As if he thought his wife was still alive. "What do you mean we're all the same?"

"Which word are you failing to grasp?"

Dakota didn't bite at the sarcasm. "I mean to say, you mention it like it's an accusation."

He snorted, still fumbling with his phone, caught between indecision. "No offense, but your gender ruins everything. You're the most entitled humans on this planet. You want to be taken care of, and you also want all the perks. You want your cake and frosting. Or whatever that saying is."

Dakota just nodded. She'd heard far worse directed at her on account of her gender. Especially from criminals. "Would it surprise you to hear that your wife is dead?"

He looked sharply up at her now, his eyes narrowing. "That's not funny."

"I'm not laughing. Sir, I really am law enforcement. I need you to lower that gun."

He looked confused, stunned. Dakota could now feel adrenaline rushing through her. Her exhaustion and sleep deprivation were quickly being replaced by a sense of uncertainty. Marcus's theory about the killer targeting vulnerable people didn't fit. Kramer's wife was a wealthy lawyer. But Mr. Kramer didn't seem to know his wife was dead. Of course, if he was as smart as she gave him credit for, then this was all an act. He was playing the role well, but she thought she detected cracks in the facade.

There was an intelligence in those eyes, though he endeavored to conceal it. He still hadn't called anyone on his phone. It didn't take that long to dial 911. He was bluffing. He had no intention of calling the cops. Why would a guilty man want law enforcement involved?

She had already identified herself a few times. And she knew she looked like an FBI agent. Her tattoos weren't visible because of her long sleeves and collar.

But he wasn't letting her show her identification. Which meant he didn't care. So he had something to hide.

And now that she had told him about his wife's death, it was nearly impossible to read his expression. Partly, he looked stunned. But also, he looked angry. This business about women being entitled suggested their marital problems had reached something of an impasse.

"Did you kill her, Mr. Kramer?" Dakota said. In her mind she could picture a past life, in the cage, shoving off her back foot, countering a punch and following up with an uppercut. She'd had enough of playing possum.

The question sent Jerry reeling. "She's dead? Wait, you really are FBI?"

"I said I was. I think you know I am. Why are you still pointing that gun at me, sir?"

His hand was trembling now. He bit his lip, swallowing, lowering the gun just a bit. "Hang on," he said quickly. "This isn't right. I'm being set up. She's dead? That bitch."

Dakota blinked at this reaction. "Your wife's death makes you angry?"

"She's doing this on purpose. She killed herself, didn't she? Made it look like I did it. Of course, she did. That bitch!" he repeated, louder, his face twisting into a snarl.

"Mr. Kramer, please calm down." She began to lower her hands, slowly.

He didn't seem to notice at first. He was shaking his head, furious. Whether he was acting or not, the news that his wife was dead certainly wasn't grieving the man. If anything, he just looked angrier.

"I knew she was going to try to screw me," he said. "But this really takes the cake. She's the sex addict. She's the one stepping out on *me*. You women are all the same!"

His voice was rising as he ranted, and his gun gesticulated one way, then the other, like a conductor's wand. Dakota noticed movement, her eyes darting to the side.

Marcus Clement was emerging around the building, weapon in hand, crouched and approaching slowly from behind.

He had a clean shot, but she gave a quick shake of her head. He kept his gun aimed but didn't squeeze the trigger.

"Mr. Kramer," Dakota said, "I'm warning you, sir. Please, lower the weapon. We can talk about this."

But the metalworker was too angry. His gun was still raised. Now, he was ranting, spittle flying, and it was as if he didn't even see her. "Women just break everything. They ruin stuff. They're like parasites, coming in to suck the blood out of hard-working, good men."

Dakota maintained her calm. “You are a good man? I would like to believe you. Let's talk about it. Lower the gun."

He was shaking his head though, his face reddening. "She did this. If she's dead. She did it. She's framing me!"

"So you admit you look guilty?"

"That's not what I said," he screeched. Suddenly, he spotted Marcus. The man yelped and took two sprinting steps away. But then, realizing that the alley would be a perfect firing range, he stumbled to the side. He flung himself against the wall, a few feet away from Dakota, using her as something of a human shield and placing her directly between Marcus and himself.

Now that he'd been spotted, Agent Clement's voice boomed out, "Sir, lower the weapon. Hands in the air. FBI!"

The man's face turned pale now. He seemed to finally realize that they hadn't been lying. "FBI?" he squeaked. "Shit. She played me. She *played* me."

"Sir, put the gun down!"

But he was as white as a sheet, and suddenly, Dakota noticed his thumb moving towards the safety.

He clicked it. The gun was live, and now was waving in her direction and towards Marcus. He was only a couple of steps away from her, and Marcus didn't have a clean shot.

She could see Kramer's shock turning to rage. "She set me up!" he was screaming. "That dead bitch set me up!"

He clearly wasn't sad about his wife's death. He wasn't calming down. He was only getting angrier.

"Dakota," Marcus said warily.

"I see it," she called back. Her eyes never left Mr. Kramer.

The gun waved one way, then the other, as he continued to shout, anger rising. Lights flicked on in the office building on the top floor, suggesting someone was either working late or squatting.

But Dakota didn't look.

She waited a second longer, the gun waving off to the side. Then, when it was aimed towards the wall, a foot to her left, she surged forward, fast.

Part of playing possum was knowing when to end the pretense. And now, the danger had reached a breaking point.

She flung her left hand out, high and wide. The movement caught his eye, caught the attention of his weapon. He raised it sharply. But at the same time, she flung her right hand towards his wrist. She hit it, hard, closing the gap between them in one lunging step.

Her fist, slamming into his wrist, sent the gun clattering. He didn't even get off a shot. The gun hit the ground, and in the same motion she kicked it away.

Now, Mr. Kramer was hissing painfully, stumbling back, and clutching his arm. Dakota took another step forward, this time bringing her elbow into his chest. He reeled back, ricocheting off the stone wall.

And like that, in a matter of seconds, the man was disarmed, and she was standing with her forearm braced against him.

Still, he was larger than her. And she wasn't prideful enough to think he would pose no threat, even unarmed. He was a metalworker. Who knew what type of weapons he might have on him; she kept her arm against him, but at the same time grabbed his wrist, the one she'd punched, and twisted, firmly, but not enough to break anything.

He yelled, but she spun him around and then locked his arm behind his back. "Marcus!" she called.

She needn't have bothered, though, as Agent Clement was sprinting towards her with thumping footsteps. She heard the rattle of handcuffs emerging as he reached her side.

"Sir," she said sharply, "stop struggling. Please stop. I'm not trying to hurt you. Just stop. We need to ask you some questions."

He was gasping, his voice hoarse as he continued to curse his wife and Dakota. With Marcus's help she cuffed him, putting his hands behind his back. Agent Clement fetched the weapon, picking it up with the edge of his shirt to avoid smudging fingerprints.

Then, the two of them hurried back towards their car; Mr. Kramer pushed ahead of them, still spluttering as he went.

CHAPTER FIFTEEN

The first few rays of sunlight trickled through the reinforced window in the interrogation room. Dakota stifled a yawn, sitting across the table from Mr. Kramer. Jerry didn't look quite so handsome under the bright lights as he had back in the alley. His eyes were puffy, his lips pale and pressed in a thin line. His fingers tapped rhythmically against the table, his handcuffs rattling. One of his feet was vibrating against the floor as he glanced nervously between the two agents.

Dakota sat upright, straight postured, eyes ahead. Marcus slouched with two empty cups in front of him, the lingering odor of coffee wafting through the room thanks to the ventilation system.

Marcus made no effort to hide his own yawn, passing a hand over his mouth and staring at the ceiling.

Dakota, deciding to keep Kramer rattled, didn't address him right away. Instead, she scanned through her phone, flicking through the images of the crime scenes.

Her phone rested on the table so, upside down, Kramer could still see what she was looking at.

Every time she caught him glancing, his face turned a different color. From red to green to white. She was having a hard time reading the man.

He had motive, means, and opportunity. He had problems with his wife, the skills to set up the crime scenes, and seven days since his neighbors had seen him.

He had pulled a weapon on the FBI and had refused to lower it even when they'd identified.

Yet, on the other hand, he seemed overwhelmed. Maybe he didn't ever think he was going to be caught.

As Dakota flipped through the images, she considered what connections their suspect had with the first two victims. He had already displayed a contempt for women. But sexism wasn't a crime. Still, a killer with disregard for the life of a female might have no qualms about killing one in order to disguise the murder of his wife.

"How do you know Caitlynn Jackson?" Dakota said suddenly, looking up as she spoke.

The man blinked. "My wife's name was Terin."

He was good. She had to hand him that. He was now using the past tense. He hadn't even batted an eyelid at the name of the first victim. She tried again.

"What about Michelle Stanton?"

He wrinkled his nose. "Who? Why am I even here? This was all a misunderstanding. I thought you were trespassers trying to steal from my shop."

Marcus leaned in now, exhaling, his breath smelling of cheap coffee. "I looked into that," he said. "You had two break-ins in the last year. You get a lot of work as a fabricator?"

The man shrugged. "I do okay." Then, as if realizing he'd been presented an opportunity, he added quickly, "But no, I don't do great. In fact, the business is going under. The only way I'm able to keep it above the water is with the money from my wife's legal practice."

Dakota said, "Your wife has a lot of money for someone who works with domestic abuse victims. It isn't traditionally seen as a lucrative field."

"She does more than that. A lot of family litigation. Divorce court," he added emphatically. "That pays. Especially in the neighborhoods we work."

Dakota shook her head. "Neighborhoods where *she* works. You aren't involved with your wife's practice."

He let out a faint grunt, shrugging. "My point," he said, "is why would I kill her? That's why I'm here, right? Because she framed me for her death."

Dakota shook her head. "Sir, I can guarantee you that your wife didn't frame you."

He snorted. "Then why am I here?"

Dakota thought back to the horrible scene in the mansion's living room. The legs wrapped in metal, the arms outstretched by bolts and steel corners. Almost like a crucifix pose. The skin cold, the deep gash across the throat. It definitely wasn't a suicide. But that didn't mean the husband was guilty.

"I needed my wife to pay for my business," he said with a shrug. "Now that she's dead, I guess there's no point in lying. The life insurance was my only hope of cashing out. With her murdered, the money goes to a charity. I'm going to be wrapped up in litigation for years if I want to even see a penny; why would I do that to myself?"

Marcus shook his head. "Sometimes a temper just gets the best of you. Is that what happened? Did she say something, Jerry?"

He shook his head emphatically. "I don't even know how she died, man. What did she do? Slit her wrists? Write something on the wall about how I did it?" He snorted. "I bet you she left a note. That whore."

Dakota ignored the rant but focused on this last part. "We heard that your wife admitted to having a sex addiction. Was that the source of your marital problems?"

He shrugged. "Not my fault she had a problem. I knew about it when we got married. Hell, I thought it was kind of kinky. Turns out, it's not. She was going to groups for it. At least there was that. But I know she was sleeping around. Why should I have stayed with someone who wasn't faithful to me?" He shook his head. "Look how it's all turned out."

Dakota frowned. "Your wife was going to a *group* for sex addiction?"

"That's what she said. For all I know that was her excuse to go meet up with her new beau."

"I see," Dakota said slowly. "What night was this group meeting?"

Marcus tensed at the question, and she felt him shoot a glance in her direction. She waited, staring firmly towards their suspect. If he noticed anything, he didn't display it. He said, "Wednesday. Wednesday nights, I think. Why?"

Dakota felt a faint prickle along her arms. Wednesday night for group. Wasn't that what Caitlynn Jackson's roommate had said? She'd been going to get help with her pill problem on *Wednesday* night.

A sudden connection where there hadn't been one before.

Now, Kramer was just muttering and cursing. "I swear I didn't do anything. She broke my heart. I'm not the bad guy here. She was the one with the problem. She was the cheat. And I need that life insurance. With her dead this way, it's her final screw you. I bet that's why she did it. To stop me from getting any of the money."

He drifted off into miserable muttering.

Dakota said. "Where were you last night?"

"At the shop. I've been sleeping there."

"Your neighbor said you were staying at a hotel."

"That's what I told him. Not going to say that I'm sleeping at my workplace. These people talk. Obviously."

Dakota shook her head. "Help me to understand. You were sleeping at your shop? You didn't know anything about your wife's death? No one messaged you? No one called?"

He shrugged. "My friends don't run in those circles. My neighbors don't have my number. Besides, it was late. And then I saw you two moving around outside and I came to investigate. And now I'm here." He said this last part sullenly.

Dakota turned her phone, spinning it a couple of times, feeling the cold metal of the table against her fingers as they skimmed past.

He made a compelling case. But she'd met liars who could convince their own mothers that the moon was made of cheese.

"Can anyone vouch for your whereabouts?"

He didn't miss a beat. "Sure. I have two employees. They went home about half an hour before you two showed up."

Marcus cleared his throat. "Around nine PM? Kind of late, isn't it? Do these employees have names?"

Jerry seemed to realize he'd hit a nerve. He leaned in. "I'll give you their phone numbers and addresses if you want. Why? When was she killed?"

Dakota sighed. If he was telling the truth, and if his employees could verify it, that meant he was clear of the murders. His workspace was too far from the mansion to have gotten there in time. Besides, to set up the horrible scene, he would've needed at least an hour.

Dakota felt a fit of frustration.

She glanced at Marcus, studying the side of his face. Her partner was also frowning. He was sleep deprived, cranky, but also had a look in his eyes that cut her to the core.

Disappointment. This wasn't their suspect. He wasn't the killer. They would have to check the alibi, of course. But it wasn't matching up. Nothing he did suggested he knew the other victims. He hated his wife, but not once had he changed his story. He still seemed to think she'd killed herself or had herself killed to frame him. And while he could be acting, it didn't match with the rest. On top of it, he had an alibi that could be verified.

She let out a deflated sigh. Marcus wasn't even looking at her now. Perhaps he was just tired, or perhaps the source of his disappointment was too much to look at.

She felt her stomach twist, felt her hand clenched on the cold table.

She needed to solve this case. She needed to figure it out, not just so she could please Agent Carter, but so she could prove Marcus right. He'd gone to bat for her; he'd gone out of his way to bring her back. And again, they were swinging and missing. She was coming up empty.

At this rate, she wasn't going to prove anything to anyone. The last thing she would get would be access to those old case files from Agent Carter. She'd be lucky if she kept her job at this pace.

She let out a long breath. Maybe the alibi wouldn't check out. Yes, that was it. Maybe he was lying. She was counting herself out too quickly.

She pushed stiffly to her feet. "You can take it from here," she said to Marcus, keeping her tone devoid of emotion. "I'll be back."

She pointed towards Kramer. "I need the names and numbers of those employees of yours. Here, write it down."

She pulled a piece of paper from the folder on the seat next to her and grabbed a pencil from where it jutted out of the binding. She rounded the table and slapped the pad and pencil in front of their suspect.

"Write," she said, trying to keep her tone in check.

Inwardly, though, she felt like she was on fire

Sleep deprived, failing at the case, feeling as if all eyes were watching her stumble, Dakota needed the alibis not to check out. She needed him to be lying.

CHAPTER SIXTEEN

Dakota sat in the stationary car as raindrops drummed against the windshield. She liked the seclusion. It gave her time to think.

She glanced through the glass at the rain clouds that had rolled quickly across the horizon. It reminded her of a case she'd once had in Seattle. In Illinois, though, the rain didn't come in spurts. When it arrived, it threatened to stay for as long as it wanted.

Water now streaked through the streets and droplets stippled the windows.

She watched sympathetically as a couple of police officers held newspapers over their heads and raced up the steps into the precinct.

Marcus was still speaking with their suspect, but she'd already texted him the bad news.

The alibi checked out. Both employees had vouched for Mr. Kramer. They could be lying, but at this point, she knew she had to think like a DA. There were too many coincidences, too many holes. Kramer wasn't their man. And if he was, he was playing them all like a fiddle.

But she couldn't think like that. She had to go back to square one. She shifted uncomfortably in the cramped passenger seat, tapping her fingers against the glass in the same rhythm as the raindrops.

A cup of coffee sat in the cup holder next to her. She smiled at it. Marcus often went out of his way to accommodate some of her stranger tendencies. Dakota didn't like keeping things neat and clean to be a ball buster. It helped her think. An uncluttered space was an uncluttered mind.

She had taken the same approach to training. Coach Little's gym was pristine, despite what happened inside the cage. She frowned, refocusing.

Wednesdays. Both Kramer and Claire had mentioned the victims had something Wednesday night. A sex addiction and a pill dependency.

Dakota shifted uncomfortably whenever this topic came to mind. She didn't think of herself as an addict. She knew that others insisted that, until she did, she could never properly recover. But in her mind, thinking of herself that way only made it harder to deny a drink.

Still, the Wednesday similarity was a connection that hadn't come up before.

She frowned and pulled her phone out, quickly dialing a number. She waited, listening to the rain, and then Marcus answered.

"More news?"

"Not with the alibi," she said quickly. "He's still clear."

Mark sighed. Was that another note of disappointment? Maybe she was just in her own head. She swallowed, trying to focus. "You okay?"

"Still in the room," Marcus said, trying to keep his tone neutral.

"My bad. Sorry. Quick question, what was the group his wife went to?"

"Give me a second."

"Take your time."

Marcus bid his farewell and hung up.

Dakota kept her phone gripped in one hand. Knowing her partner, it wouldn't take long for him to get the information she needed. He had always been good with people, good with talking. It only took a couple of minutes for her phone to buzz.

A text message. She glanced down.

Community Center on Chase Street. Wednesday nights.

Dakota felt a flicker of excitement.

If she could find where the killer was hunting his victims, then she might be able to find the killer before he struck again. She accessed the web browser on her phone, cycling to the community center in question.

It took her a few seconds of navigating the old, outdated website to find the group meetings. She scanned the information for Wednesday night. At first, she didn't think it was listed. But then, at the bottom of the page, she spotted a name. Dr. Donna Bristol. Recovery counselor. A phone number was listed.

Dakota called it.

She waited, the speaker on, her phone flat in front of her face.

A few seconds passed, and then a voice responded, "Dr. Bristol speaking."

Dakota said, "Umm, hello. Dr. Bristol? My name is Agent Steele. I'm with the FBI. I was wondering if you could answer some questions for me."

"Is this a joke?" the voice said. A professional, lighthearted tone. A voice that didn't take itself too seriously, and yet somehow communicated an air of competence.

"I'm afraid it's not a joke. I can send you a picture of my badge if you'd like."

"Mhmm. You'd best tell me what this is about."

"It's about the recovery groups at the community center. They're not listed online. It's just your name."

A pause, and Dakota knew the woman was trying to decide if she should continue the conversation over the phone. Then, Bristol said, "Actually do you mind showing me that ID?"

"No problem." Dakota held up her ID, covering irrelevant details, but allowing the picture and the FBI logo to speak for itself—she took a picture, and sent it.

A few moments passed, and then the voice on the other line said, "Goodness! What's this about?"

No sense mincing words. Dakota just came out and said it, "I'm afraid two women from your Wednesday night groups were murdered."

A sharp intake of breath. "You're joking."

"I'm afraid not. Terin Kramer was killed last night. Two nights before, Caitlynn Jackson was murdered"

"Oh my God," said Dr. Bristol.

The tone was one of recognition. Dakota felt her heart skip. "You knew them?"

"Yes, yes of course. I worked with both of them. I coordinate the groups at the center. We don't post them online in order to avoid attracting the wrong sorts."

"The wrong sorts?"

The doctor sighed. "For a couple of years, we were attracting people who enjoyed fetishizing grief and addiction. It was this horrible debacle. We found more success advertising by word-of-mouth and in the center itself. The groups are thriving. I didn't know that those women had been killed."

Dakota winced. "I'm sorry to tell you like this." The rain seemed to pick up. Thunder threatened in the background with a growl. Dakota leaned back in the seat. "I actually need to ask you about another woman."

"Dear Lord, *another* one? Are the people in our group safe?"

"I don't know yet. Did you know someone by the name of Michelle Stanton?"

A pause. "I—I'm not sure. You're sure that's her name?"

"I'm sure. Maybe she entered the group under a pseudonym."

"Maybe," the doctor said doubtfully. "Could you maybe describe her to me?"

"I can do you better. I'll send a picture."

Dakota cycled to the second victim's file, took a screenshot of her face, and texted it. A few seconds passed, and then the woman on the other line said, "I have no clue who this is. She doesn't attend either of our groups."

"You have different groups?"

"Different needs. Some for sexual dependency, others for chemical. It changes depending on who signs up in the need of the moment."

Dakota frowned, that sense of anticipation from earlier fading now. "You're sure that woman didn't attend?"

"I'm reading through our sign-ups now. She didn't. I don't recognize her. There's no one by the name of Michelle. No one with that last name. No, I'm quite positive she doesn't attend."

Dakota pressed her teeth together. "*Did* she perhaps? Is there a chance she attended a few months ago, maybe a year ago?"

"I've been on staff here for five years. I don't recognize her. I would have, too; she looks a bit like my sister. I'm sorry, agent. But I don't know this woman."

Dakota let out a huff of frustration but tried to hide it as an exhalation. "All right, thank you. I appreciate your time."

"Hang on, agent—are the people in our group safe? Should we cancel for the week?"

Dakota considered this. She said, "It might be smart, just to be safe."

"God, I don't know what I'm going to say. Alright, well, thank you for letting me know. Erm, not to intrude, but you haven't—I mean to say, the one who's doing this isn't—"

"We don't have him yet," Dakota cut in. She wanted to add more. Wanted to act like they were getting close. Wanted to give some sense of comfort or encouragement. But it would've been a lie. They weren't close to catching the killer at all. She had no clue who was doing this.

"I'm very sorry—I have to go," Dakota said.

She hung up. She sat in the car under the gray skies, the parking lot having been rapidly cleared by the rain. Thunder continued to grumble in the background with a guttural snarl.

Dakota felt her own growl warming. She'd missed it. The victims were not connected by the same group. So what connected them? It couldn't have been a coincidence, could it?

Dakota let out a long sigh.

She wasn't thinking straight. Sleep deprived, exhausted, she just wanted to lean back and...

The anxiety was getting too much. The pressure to succeed, to not let anyone down, it was immense. It felt like she would collapse.

Normally, she would cope. But how could she cope when she couldn't drink, and she couldn't catch the killer? Part of her, for a wild moment, wondered if there were any gyms nearby. A couple of rounds in a cage would clear her head.

But she couldn't abandon the investigation in the middle of it. With shaking hands, she cycled through her phone to find Coach Little's number.

She dialed, waiting as the phone rang. How many times in the past had she contacted the Irishman? The father figure she'd never had. The only man who'd ever taken an interest when she'd been younger. At least, the sort of interest she'd wanted.

As her phone rang, though, she hung up just as quickly. He was probably working with someone. Coach Little was always working. There were others in the community who needed him far more than she did. She sighed, shot off a quick text: *Sorry for calling. Everything's fine.*

She sent it, and then shoved her phone into her pocket.

As she did, the device vibrated.

She yanked it back out, excited.

The coach?

No. She frowned. Not quite in disappointment.

It was a text from Agent Mark Bonet, the good-looking techie. A simple text. A smiley face. Followed by: *I found this new taco place I think you might like.*

She bit her lip. It wasn't a date. Obviously it wasn't a date. Why would he be asking her on a date? He knew how her career had collapsed. He knew she was on Agent Carter's shit list.

Of course, he didn't want to date...

And yet as she read the message, the smiley face, the gentle reminder about his offer to take her out, she couldn't help but feel a strange sense of sadness.

These were the sorts of texts she wished she could enjoy. A handsome tech worker back at the office? What was there to dislike?

She tried to smile, thinking of the way his eyes brightened whenever he told a joke. His sense of humor.

She frowned, lowering the phone again.

Then, in a spurt of anger she deleted the message and pushed her phone back in her pocket.

She couldn't allow herself to be distracted. The case needed her attention. Her happiness took a backseat to solving this thing. She couldn't be selfish. Besides, it wasn't a date. He wasn't interested. Why would he be?

Are you *interested?* a small, niggling voice whispered.

She scowled at the thought.

It wasn't a fair question.

As she sat there, considering her options, she frowned. There was one other thing she could try.

CHAPTER SEVENTEEN

He swiped through the news app on his phone, a scowl on his face. They weren't displaying his latest work... His fingers tightened on the device, and he stamped his foot in frustration. Why in the hell weren't they showing his work?

A few articles mentioned something about a murder in an expensive neighborhood, but none of them had pictures of his creation. Why? Didn't they see what he was doing?

He hissed in frustration, standing in the large hallway by one of the water fountains. A couple of onlookers slipped by, glancing in his direction. As they passed, they shot him another look and then quickly broke into whispering which they didn't seem to think (or care if) he heard.

He ignored them. He was used to being watched. He'd put in a lot of work for his physique after all.

Once, he'd been like *them.* Like his subjects. His muses.

But by his own hand, by his own effort and hard work, he'd become something else... Something greater.

Why couldn't they see he was doing the same thing? Those women were useless without him. Meaningless, small, pathetic entities who needed his help. He was purging them of their helplessness. Couldn't they see that? Why didn't anyone care?

He exhaled shakily, closing his eyes and leaning against the water fountain. The backs of his knuckles grazed the cold metal.

He felt a faint flicker of calm return. He knew metal. Metal was his friend. The job he'd been given out of prison had been working in a shop. It was what had set him on the path to figuring out his life—no. No—*he* had set *himself* on the path.

He nodded to himself, eyes still closed, considering just how far he'd brought himself.

He was stronger than these ones. Than his muses. But he could see the beauty in all of them, the perfection that just needed a little coaxing to bring out.

And his latest model? Near perfection.

She'd been a slut. A horrible little whore, but now... now she was ascendant. Now she was free from her affliction. That other little creature? The one with the pill addiction. A horrible, evil little habit.

He wrinkled his nose in disgust, his mind flitting back to moments of his own failing sobriety.

A flash of fury arose in him as he considered his own failures in the past. But no more! Not again! He'd cured himself!

The vestiges from the bolt of rage still circled his system, and his hand gripped the edge of the water fountain. His fingers strained, tightening, his teeth grinding. He wasn't like that anymore. No—no it wasn't even him. He'd never been that. He'd been possessed. Controlled. It wasn't his fault.

These people, though—these failures *needed* him to save them.

He opened his eyes, his fingers still tensed against the water fountain. He had to remember why he was here. An artist was never appreciated until they'd completed a body of work, after all. The last one had been buried, hidden in some C-class news articles. But this new masterpiece?

His new muse would change everything.

Not just one this time. *Two.* Sisters.

It was why he'd come here, after all. Normally, he didn't like crowds.

Ahead, he watched as the two figures who'd giggled at him pushed through double doors, stepping into a large conference room. Beyond, he spotted the convention in full swing. Tables were set up displaying sculptures of wood and clay, baskets woven of old refuse and silk threads.

His eyes darted quickly around the room, around the hundred or more people milling throughout the space.

He'd never been too good with numbers. But *two* was easy enough to figure. And the two new muses weren't in the woodworking or clay section. No—he could see them at the far end of the room, setting up on the stage.

Metalworkers, fabricators like himself. Artistic in their own right. As he thought it, though, his lip curled. Hacks. Both of them.

No one knew their dirty little secret. No one except him. They'd tried for years to figure it out but had never managed. So, he was here to help.

He stood near the water fountain, fingers tight, sweat beading on his forehead. He wasn't *scared.* Of course not. Definitely not nervous. He just didn't like crowds. Too many people—too many threats. Too many desperate souls in need of his tender mercies.

Yes, that was it. The crowds needed him.

He nodded to himself, pushing off the wall, releasing his grip on the water fountain and taking a step towards those open double doors. The two figures slipped through, allowing the door to swing slowly shut behind them.

The sound of milling guests, the gentle hubbub faded. He picked up his pace, ramming his hands into his pockets, and frowning as he marched forward. As he drew near, the door swung open again, nearly catching him across the face.

He jerked back, avoiding the collision just in time.

An older man with a woman on his arm stepped through. "Oh my," the man said, glancing up at the craftsman. "Aren't you a big fella. Here for the show?"

He received no response. Responses were for the worthy. The craftsman sidestepped the weakling and his wife, stepping into the room.

His stomach twisted as he did. The man had a belly—gluttony. His arms were small—weakness. His dopey grin was all too pathetic. And the way he'd stepped back to let the craftsman pass? Cowardice.

He turned, scowling after the two figures as the door shut again.

He couldn't solve everyone's problems, though. It would take forever. No—he had to focus. One issue at a time.

As he moved further into the convention hall, he tried to stick to the wall, skirting the outside of the space, avoiding as many of the onlookers as possible. People were oohing and aahing over subpar works, purchasing mediocre wares wherever he looked.

Ahead, on the stage, though, he spotted one of his muses.

The woman was a few years older than him but had pleasant features. Her twin sister's hair was dyed darker, but otherwise they were the spitting image of each other. They even wore the same sweaters advertising their booth.

Why in the hell the convention had chosen to highlight *their* creations was beyond him. He'd submitted his own application fifteen times. They hadn't even let him in on the floor.

Sheer jealousy, of course.

He shook his head in pity at how moronic the convention organizers were. No matter, he was here now anyway. They'd treated him poorly, but he had come to provide a favor.

He picked up his pace, moving around the edge of the booths, behind chairs and backs facing him. A few of the people shot him interested looks, as was customary, given his notable appearance.

He smiled at this. Not at *them,* but at their attention.

All the while, moving through the room, slowly approaching the stage. A few of these people he recognized from other local art shows. Some of them he'd shared booths with, in the past, at smaller conventions. He didn't like any of them, and certainly would never associate with them outside of studio time.

"Lauren!" a voice called.

He looked up, watching as one of his muses turned on the stage, glancing back towards one of the exits. Another woman, with darker hair, was trying to pull a large metal container through the door. She was huffing and grunting, her face red. He smirked at how she struggled.

"Lauren, come help!" the sister shouted, slapping a hand against the container which emitted a tinny sound.

The sister on the stage sighed, no longer adjusting the items on the long table, but stepping past a podium and hopping off the stage to go help her sister.

His two muses, both in one spot.

He'd thought this particular piece through for a while. He knew what he had to do.

He picked up his pace, forcing a smile across his features. "Need some help?" he called out, cheerfully.

The two women looked up at him, eyes widening slightly and tilting their heads as he approached.

"Sure," the one called Lauren said instantly. "And what's *your* name?"

He kept smiling, reaching out a hand in greeting. "Oh, I suppose it depends on who you ask. Here, just step outside and push. I'll lift from here."

The sisters shrugged and moved to the other side of the metal container. Both of them now stood on the other side of the exit door.

It might have been the perfect opportunity. But no—he'd already planned. He knew what he had to do.

Never deviate from the sketch, never ignore the reference model. It had worked so far, and he wasn't about to change it now.

He just kept smiling and then, with one arm, lifted the metal piece, receiving due praise in the form of small gasps of delight and compliments.

Par for the course.

The two of them didn't know just how lucky they were.

He hefted the metal container, dragging it into the convention, his newest muses dragging behind.

CHAPTER EIGHTEEN

Dakota stood in the lobby of the hotel next to Marcus as he finished checking in at the desk.

"Dakota?" he was saying, tapping her arm. "Earth to Dakota—Steele, can you hear me?"

She blinked, turning to regard where her partner was leaning against the faux-wood counter. The look of disappointment from earlier was no longer visible. Knowing Marcus, she was probably just getting stuck in the weeds of her own thoughts. Clement wasn't the type to think poorly of his partners. But she couldn't shake the feeling that she was failing.

Which was why, now, she was pacing uncomfortably on the laminate floor of the cheap two-star hotel. She glanced down where his hand was tapping her wrist, his other arm cocked to support his weight against the counter. The clerk was watching them both curiously. She supposed it was somewhat unusual for patrons to check into a hotel so early in the morning.

But her pulse was racing, taking her mind on a trip with it. She had another angle and was still trying to tease it out. Her phone was clutched in her left hand, displaying the most recent search results.

"Oh, sorry," she said, returning her attention to Marcus's searching gaze. She could just about glimpse her own reflection in the glass of his spectacles which illuminated the lights above. The left side of her partner's glasses was slightly smudged. Marcus didn't seem to notice. It was only a sliver of fog against the glass, but it still made her uncomfortable.

She hesitated, then reached out with her sleeve, wincing, "Umm—mind if—no just... here." She quickly wiped it clear and lowered her hand.

Marcus just blinked owlishly at her. "Thank you," he said after a moment. "But I was wondering if you wanted to get some rest before getting back at it? It's been a very, very long night..."

Dakota hesitated, trying to pick up anything in her partner's tone, but he carried his usual friendly demeanor accompanied by an ever-accommodating tone.

She needed accommodating given what she was thinking.

"I—I think I'm onto something," she said suddenly, pulling her arm back from his and turning towards her phone again. She lifted it, showing it towards Agent Clement. "These are all the support groups within walking distance of that abandoned trainyard."

Marcus blinked. He exhaled faintly, his nostrils flaring. He reached up, adjusting his glasses, and smudging the very edge in the same spot as before. This time, Dakota bit her tongue and tried not to look at it. Appearances mattered, cleanliness mattered—but if she tried to adjust every misplaced lamp or untucked shirt, she'd go insane.

So instead, she looked determinedly down at her phone again. "I think this might be the angle. All of these groups meet Wednesday night."

"Hang on—these are the same groups that you called about—"

"No—no, none of these take place in the community center," she said quickly, shaking her head. "But I was thinking."

"Always a good start."

"Har har. But maybe the women didn't all go to the *same* group. Maybe they weren't associated. But the coordinator at the community center mentioned something about members showing up who fetishized grief and recovery. People who didn't belong in the groups but came just to look. She said it was a debacle. That's why they don't advertise anymore."

Marcus sighed. "I think I've reached a conclusion of my own, actually."

"Oh? What?"

"I'm not going to get any rest today, am I?"

Dakota patted the big man on the arm. "You've suffered worse," she said in what she hoped was an encouraging tone. Inflection had always been an elusive muse. "Remember New Jersey?"

"We both remember Jersey."

She smirked but sobered just as quickly. "Look—I think this might be it. Our second victim, Michelle Stanton, didn't have a car. Didn't have a bus pass. She didn't have money for a taxi. And as far as we can find, she didn't have any close associates. At least not since she moved here from Indiana."

Marcus, conceding that he wouldn't be able to sleep for the moment, was frowning now as he considered the words, nodding as he listened. "I see," he said slowly. "So you think that Michelle might have been attending a group?"

“At the trainyard I spotted a bunch of smashed bottles outside the gate.”

“That could've been anyone.”

“Yes—yes of course. But there were other bottles near that tent of hers. What if she had a drinking problem?”

“That's a reach, Steele.”

“Not really. Not completely. A beautiful, young woman like that living in an abandoned trainyard? Something went wrong.”

“It could have been any number of things.”

Dakota waved her phone to emphasize her point. “I know that! But something connects the victims, Clement. Something ties them together. I think it's Wednesday night. It's too much of a coincidence.” Dakota blinked, realizing now she'd been raising her voice. She cleared her throat uncomfortably and resumed a placating posture after an uncomfortable glance towards the hotel clerk who was watching them in fascination. She took a step to the side if only to hide in Marcus's illustrious shadow.

“Alright, so you think Stanton attended a group on Wednesdays. There's no way for us to know which one.”

“That's just it!” Dakota crowed, raising her phone again. “There aren't that many support groups for AA within walking distance of that trainyard.”

Marcus' eyes brightened. “I see...” he murmured. “So you think she was limited by her means of transportation.”

“It makes sense. Wouldn't she have been?”

Marcus nodded. “So what? You think the killer is just targeting addicts wherever he finds them?”

“Maybe... Maybe...” Dakota murmured. She glanced back at her phone, turning a bit so Marcus could also see the results while concealing them from the hotel clerk. She shot a look towards the man. “Do you mind?” she said testily.

Marcus winced. “Sorry,” he added on her behalf.

The clerk sniffed and turned, pretending to busy himself with a computer. The faint tap of clacking keys behind them sufficiently camouflaged Dakota's next comment. Her foot squeaked against the tiled floor as she shifted in excitement.

“I've found three that would fit the bill.”

“Three?” Marcus said, surprised. “All in the same walking radius?”

Dakota pressed her lips together. “AA is more prevalent than you might think,” she said simply.

Marcus didn't reply, but he did place a hand lightly on her shoulder in a supportive gesture. He lowered it a second later, focused intently on the phone if only to reroute the conversation on her behalf. “Ah,” he said, “so these are the three?”

“Yes. St. Wesley's church on President's Ave. And then here we have Leksian Brothers—a local outpatient clinic. And here's a publicly advertised meetup on one of those social websites.”

Marcus studied each one, tapping a finger to his lips. “What are the odds our killer was an outpatient too?”

“Probably not as high as the other two. There'd be less vetting, far less information required upfront. No health insurance. No ID. The church or the meet-up would let anyone attend. At least, that's what the websites seem to suggest.”

Marcus clicked his tongue softly. “I think... you might be onto something. Alright,” he said at last, nodding. “Want to split up and take them separately?”

Dakota hesitated but shook her head. “The problem here is that the clinic and the meet-up both have listed phone numbers, but the church expects you to meet in person. I'm guessing it's for church attendees.”

“Do we know if Ms. Stanton was religious?”

Dakota gave a brief shake of her head. “No... But we need to track that one down in person. As for the other two, how about you take the meet-up and I'll call the clinic—”

As her excitement mounted and she spoke hurriedly, Dakota was suddenly cut off by a faint buzzing noise. She blinked in surprise and a second later, her phone began to vibrate in her fingers. She nearly dropped it in surprise.

Then, when she saw the number, her stomach plummeted.

“Shit,” she muttered.

Marcus swallowed uncomfortably at the cuss word.

“It's Agent Carter,” Dakota whispered. She paused, for one wild moment wondering if she could just let it go to voicemail. But then, with a sigh, she realized this might only exacerbate the issue and so she lifted the device, trying to keep her tone neutral.

“Hello?” Dakota said.

“Agent Steele?” the voice on the other end said curtly. It might have just been Dakota's imagination, but Carter had a way of communicating that made her feel as if she were being perpetually summoned to the principal's office. She had a lot of experience with that very thing.

“Yes, ma'am. Agent Carter?”

"Yes..." the voice trailed off. "You have my number saved, don't you?"

"I—yes... Sorry. I know it's you. Just..." Dakota went silent, waiting and wincing.

Carter seemed to let the silence linger a bit longer than necessary, but then at last said, "Why is the local sergeant under the impression that you two might be unreachable?"

"I—what?"

"He said that he thought you would be sleeping, given your long night. Why is the local police sergeant," she said, enunciating each word with crisp precision, "under the impression that you'd be sleeping this late in the morning."

Dakota glanced at the clock on her phone. It was only 8 AM. But she decided this wasn't a point worth quibbling over. Marcus coughed, though, leaning in and wincing. "Sorry Agent Carter. That was my fault. I mentioned we hadn't slept the previous night and to make sure to contact us with emergencies."

"I see," said Agent Carter. Now that she was speaking to Marcus, her tone seemed softer. "Perfectly understandable, Clement, but it looks as if the locals' definition of an emergency and yours might be different."

Marcus blinked. "Apologies, ma'am?"

"No need to apologize. But there's been another murder. They wanted me to contact you. I was given the impression that they were somewhat... intimidated by you."

Marcus sighed, passing a hand over his face. This wasn't the first time Clement's giant size alone had altered professional conduct. "I told them to call me with emergencies," he said in a world-weary voice. "I'm sorry they roped you into it, ma'am."

Dakota was leaning in, though, her brow creased. "Another murder, Agent Carter?"

"Yes." The tone went colder. "Two actually. Are you and Clement at the hotel now?"

"Yes ma'am."

"You're not sleeping together, are you?"

Dakota's eyes widened and she spluttered. Marcus said, "We were just checking in, ma'am."

"Good. You know office policy about fraternization. Now I need you both to head to this convention center."

"A convention center?" Dakota said grateful to slip rapidly past the previous comment. Apparently, no boundaries were off limits with Agent Carter. Intrusiveness wasn't high on Dakota's *like-me* list. She could feel her own temper threatening to rise but at the same time knew she had to keep herself in check if she wanted a chance of accessing those old case files. Besides, at this point, she'd do what was necessary to get into the boss's good graces.

"Some sort of exhibition of art and ceramics amidst other sorts of things," said Agent Carter. "I'm not clear. I've sent both of you the address. You'd better hurry."

"Do they still have the body in place?" Dakota asked quickly.

"Bodies," Agent Carter said. "Two of them. This time it was a double homicide. This is going to turn to national news soon, dammit!" Her tone hardened. "Marcus," she said. "Is... is your *help* not sufficient?"

Clement frowned, preparing to answer, but Carter cut him off. "Never mind. Look, just get going—keep your phones on this time." She hung up without so much as a farewell.

Dakota stood there, her skin prickling. "Two?" she murmured.

Marcus was already moving, fishing the car keys from his pocket as he hastened towards the spinning front door to the hotel. Dakota followed after him, her stomach twisting.

As Marcus reached the door, he paused, seemed to be considering something, then glanced back, wincing. "Sorry about that," he said. "I told them to contact us for emergencies. I did."

"I know," Dakota said, patting his arm. "I believe you. Forget about it. If it wasn't one thing it would be another. Agent Carter is testing my guard. That's it. She's the bigger fighter."

Marcus seemed relieved that Dakota wasn't upset. He pushed through the glass door and Dakota hastened behind him. Inwardly, though, her mind was racing.

While it was true that Carter was testing Dakota's defenses. Was attacking from different angles just to see what the younger agent was made of, Dakota wasn't sure she could withstand the flurry. Eventually, in almost any cage fight, if unable to get a shot in of your own, the temptation to throw in the towel could become unbearable.

But now, they had a far bigger problem to focus on. *Two* problems.

A double homicide. Double shit.

Dakota's teeth rubbed tightly against each other as she and Marcus both broke into a jog, hastening towards the parking lot, the sound of the keys in Marcus's hand jangling as they ran.

CHAPTER NINETEEN

The large convention center loomed against the clearing skies. The rain hesitated now above Chicago's skyline, hidden in a few dark clouds, and Dakota hastened towards the large, gray building which resembled something of a warehouse in an industrial district. Figures were moving through the doors. Many of them had already reached parked cars in the lot, but remained by their vehicles, or sitting within, eyes on the building.

She could hear the faint hiss of whispered conversation and murmurings from the onlookers in the parking lot.

Through the open front doors, she spotted a strange array of tables, laden with ceramics and clay sculptures. Police officers stationed outside the doors were holding people at bay, gesturing for them to return to the parking lot. She could hear them issuing instructions but couldn't quite make out the content.

"Officer Lanzig is waving to us," Marcus said from her side. She followed his indicating finger to spot an older officer standing on the edge of the large building, behind traffic cones and caution tape and even one sawhorse. It was the same man Marcus had been speaking to back at the third victim's house. She hadn't caught his name that time.

She frowned. While there were police outside the convention centers' doors, most of the traffic from law enforcement seemed to be moving around the side of the building. She spotted paramedics and an ambulance right next to the sawhorse. Police and detectives hastened quickly over the caution tape, along the small pathway lined by trees. A couple of onlookers tried to get a better angle to take photos with their smartphones but were chased away by shouting cops.

Dakota picked up her pace, hurrying beneath the morning sunlight towards Officer Lanzig.

Judging by the number of cars in the parking lot, the convention had been in full swing. What was it that Agent Carter had said? This was an artistic exhibition? Something like that. Which meant the killer had struck in the morning. The other crimes had been committed at night.

He was escalating. His last victim had only been the previous day.

Murders back-to-back meant he was only picking up speed.

Dakota picked up her own pace, hastening along the cobblestone, towards the small walkway and beneath fluttering leaves on small branches from the saplings lining the sidewalk.

She angled along the side of the convention center, towards the back of the building where most of the foot traffic was gathered.

As she moved, her footsteps clapping against the stone path, she could feel her anticipation rising.

Two victims. That's what she'd been told. He wasn't just escalating timeframe, but also body count. This was quickly getting out of hand.

"Careful," Marcus cautioned. He prodded her to the side to avoid a group from forensics hastening past, moving in the same direction as them towards the crime scene.

They rounded the edge of the building, peering into the back space.

First, Dakota spotted the wall. High enough to hide the exit door in the back. There was a loading truck parked askew over a curb. The truck's front door was open. The lights were still blinking. No driver.

The wall across from the exit would have provided sufficient privacy...

But privacy for what?

Dakota's gaze landed on the most recent victims.

Her stomach flipped and then migrated to her toes. Shit. She pressed her teeth firmly together. Nausea and anger competed for dominance.

Two victims, both with metal braces over their hands, attaching one hand to the other. Their feet were connected by metal brackets as well. Their bodies were bent outward by a collection of rebar like a segment of bicycle spokes. The image was of a circle, the woman's protruding bodies serving as each half of the round shape. Their heads lolled to the side, their throats slit. The blood spattered the cement beneath the truck. More blood by the small dumpster against the wall.

The circle, formed from the two bodies interlocked by metal and bars, was positioned against the wall, out of the line of sight from the exit door.

The women were older than the first two victims had been, likely in their thirties.

Also, judging by the blood, they had been killed on site.

Dakota shook her head, glancing towards the truck, which was also stained and crimson.

"He did it out in the open," she said, breathlessly. "Anyone could've seen. How did he isolate them?"

Marcus was pointing towards the exit. "The only access point would've been here, or the path we just took. The sawhorse was here when we arrived."

"You think the convention blocked off that path?" She glanced back from where they'd come, eyes tracing the cobblestone beneath the saplings.

He nodded.

Dakota turned back to regard the exit, and then her eyes moved towards a large metal pill-shaped thing set to the side of the door.

"What's that?" she said.

Officer Lanzig, who'd been speaking to Marcus, cleared his throat and volunteered, "Some of the stall-tenders suggested it was part of the art exhibit for the sisters. When we arrived on scene it was blocking the exit so no one could get through."

Dakota stared. The killer had somehow secluded his two victims, killed them, blocked the door, and then had the nerve to count on a simple, stupid wooden sawhorse to keep any onlookers from stumbling upon his horrible spectacle. How many minutes had it taken for him to set up his scene?

He wasn't just a psychopath; he was a narcissist. Confident he could get away with anything. Not just murder, but brash, out in the open, double homicide in the middle of the morning.

Under the sun.

And worse still—he'd been right... No one had seen a thing.

She was beginning to *truly* hate this guy... and maybe not *just* hate. Fear was creeping in. He'd killed *two* victims during a damn convention in the morning. She'd never seen such gall on a case. She wasn't sure she'd even heard of a killer *this* brash.

"Marcus, look at the blood."

"I saw it. They were killed here. No second site this time."

Dakota let out a shaking breath. "No cameras?"

"None," said the police officer. "We've already checked."

"What about the convention guests? Did they see anything?"

The officer shook his head. "We're still interviewing people, but nothing's come up yet. We have a few still waiting back by the stage inside if you want to speak with them."

Dakota nodded once. She wasn't sure what they would've seen. The killer was so brash, so confident he would get away with it. Was she missing something?

Dakota shifted uncomfortably, trying to think it through. What did it all mean? Why was the killer escalating? Was she wrong about Wednesday night groups?

She glanced around the crime scene, trying not to look directly at the bodies. The same murder weapon most likely. Deep cuts across the throat. The killer was experienced with his blade. How had he gotten both of them, though? Had he snuck up on one while the other wasn't looking? Why hadn't anyone heard anything?

She approached the metal sculpture with the twisted bodies, forcing herself to look closer.

The flesh was untouched. No blemishes on the skin save the cuts. Nothing to suggest there had been an altercation. Again, no defensive wounds. The killer didn't want to harm his victims. At least not after death.

Strange.

She leaned in, peering at the rebar. Again, she spotted where it had been melted together, where certain scraps had been twisted, beaten, and formed into the desired shapes to lock the sisters' hands together.

Their feet had also been bound by cylinders of steel.

The metal didn't look like anything Dakota recognized or that one might pick up at a hardware store. The killer was probably making everything custom. Again, she thought back to Mr. Kramer. But the metalworker had an alibi.

She moved around the back of the truck, glancing at the ground, searching for something, anything. A discarded cigarette, a footprint, a condom...

But nothing stood out. People had been traipsing over this place for the last hour by the looks of things.

She shook her head, forcing herself to look away from the corpses.

Marcus was standing by the exit door, waiting for her. She sighed, then shrugged.

Sometimes, the clues just didn't make sense. Why was he taking such good care of the bodies?

He bled them out, and then treated them like pieces of art. Almost as if he didn't think he was harming them. But if he didn't think he was harming them, what did he think he was doing?

Helping?

She tapped her foot against the ground, staring towards the truck's back wheel parked on the curb.

"We know whose vehicle this is?" she called out.

Lanzig looked over, nodding, "It belongs to Lauren Astelay—one of the victims. Some of the convention-goers recognized it. We ran the plates. No traffic tickets. No violations. Everything up to date."

Dakota nodded, looking away. She tried to piece it together. A truck, haphazardly parked. One of these metal pieces for their sculpture placed next to the door. But there was more room in the truck bed for more pieces. The other parts of their creation were likely already inside the center. Which meant they had been in the middle of unloading their poorly parked vehicle.

The killer had struck while they'd been unloading. Had he offered to help? Had he snuck up from behind?

He had chosen the perfect moment, when they were out back, with no witnesses around.

It would've taken guts, would've taken nerves of steel, but he had clearly planned it. Another thing.

The circle they formed, as bizarre and grotesque as it was, didn't resemble the other sculptures. Was it because there were two bodies?

She let out a shaking breath, then approached Marcus by the doors. She glanced through the exit, towards the stage.

There were more tables, with sculptures, pots, odd creations. On the stage there were different chunks of metal, like a giant game of Tetris.

Three figures shifted uncomfortably against the wooden platform, trying not to look like they were staring through the exit.

Dakota stepped into the center and Marcus followed. Over her shoulder, she said, "Let's keep this door closed please."

And then she began to march across the warehouse floor towards the waiting witnesses.

CHAPTER TWENTY

It was a long space between the exit and the stage. Neither Dakota nor Marcus spoke as they hastened forward. Sometimes, even in their line of work, they just needed a few moments to process.

Dakota's one hand had balled into a fist at her side out of pure instinct. But as much as she wished for it, there was nothing for her to punch. She shot a look towards her partner.

Marcus's jaw was clenched, his hands tight at his sides as he walked stiff-legged around the table covered in glass trinkets and approached their witnesses.

Two men looked like they had color coordinated their outfits. Both wore green sweaters and bright yellow pants. One of them was bald, with glasses, while the other had an inch-tall mohawk. They were both shifting uncomfortably, their eyes ringed red.

Next to them was an older woman who couldn't have been younger than seventy. She had bright, intelligent eyes, and fluffy, curling white hair without a single strand out of place. Her pink cardigan was neat, symmetrical, without wrinkles.

Immediately, Dakota liked her.

"Can we go now?" the man with the mohawk asked, a whimper to his voice. His nametag read, *Rowley.*

Dakota shook her head. Marcus, with better bedside manner, said, "We were hoping to ask you a few questions before. Would that be okay?"

Rowley sighed. The other man patted him on the shoulder. The old woman, though, with a nametag that said *Sylvia,* had a steely look to her gaze. Sylvia snapped, "What's going on? Is it true that Lauren and Sophie are dead?"

Marcus nodded. Dakota hadn't even caught their names yet.

"You knew them?" Marcus asked.

The two men were sobbing; the old woman nodded fiercely. "We all knew them. We're a tight community. A *small* community. What happened to them?" Her eyes flashed. "Was it rape? It's always rape."

Dakota frowned. "There's no sign of sexual assault. I was wondering if you saw anything. We were told you three operated booths."

The old woman nodded. She pointed towards the table with the glass trinkets. "That one's mine. It gives me a good view of the stage. I think I spotted Sophie stacking something earlier in the morning. But I never saw her leave."

Dakota turned towards Rowley. He had cleared his tears now. He sniffed and tugged at a plastic button on his shirt, and said, "I didn't see them. I only just arrived when the police showed up and told us we had to leave. We were stopped along with a few others in order to talk with investigators. It's like I told them, we don't know anything. We didn't even know anyone had died until about ten minutes ago! It's just so awful and horrible and *ohmygosh...* I hate it."

Marcus chimed in, "I'm very sorry about that."

Dakota kept on track. "I don't mean to upset you, but we're trying to get some help on this one. The killer used metal in his attack."

"Dear God," the other man gasped. "He killed them with metal?"

"Not exactly. He made a sculpture. Like some of the tables I see here. Which one is yours?"

Rowley pointed towards a display near the stage. It had a couple of cardboard boxes on top which hadn't yet been unpacked. "We sell tin soldiers," he said. "But we create them in the likeness of the guests."

The other man, who hadn't spoken yet, nodded.

Dakota said, "All right, so maybe you can help me. It's not going to be pretty, but I need you to look at some pictures and tell me if you recognize the work."

"Dakota," Marcus cautioned. "You think it's advisable we do that here?"

She shrugged. She pointed at the stage. "Feel free to take a seat. They're not nice pictures." Then, she added, "This is a serial case. These photos are of previous victims."

Both men shifted uncomfortably, but the older woman just sniffed.

Dakota withdrew her phone, pulling up images of the last three crime scenes. She extended the device towards the men, swiping through. "I'll try not to show the bodies; I'm more interested in the metalwork. It seems strange the killer struck when he knew Sophie and Lauren would be out back. It suggests to me he has familiarity with this place. Maybe with some of you."

The old woman clicked her tongue in disapproval. "It's all that damn television," she said. "People don't work with their hands like they used to."

Dakota said, "Actually, our killer does. Well, do you recognize anything about this?"

She swiped through the photos of the different metal fastenings and creations. Occasionally there would be a glimpse of a hand or part of a leg where the photos had been zoomed in. Whenever there was a glimpse of a corpse, the three booth tenders would stiffen, shifting uncomfortably.

But, to their credit, they paid close attention, scrutinizing each passing image.

After a bit, Rowley ran a hand through his mohawk, and shook his head. "I can't say I recognize the work. It's actually pretty shoddy craftsmanship. He didn't even completely bind these two female couplings. Look here, it's the completely wrong metal—he tried to use an alloy. It wouldn't last for a week if strained."

As he spoke, the man in the matching sweater leaned in as well, frowning. The two of them began pointing out different flaws, nitpicking as if they were judges in an art show.

Dakota waited patiently. "So you're saying whoever did this is an amateur?"

They both looked up. "I'm not saying that," Rowley said. "There's a lot of professionals that do shoddy work. I'm just saying *he's* not very good. Definitely not an artist. Maybe he works on hinges." He nodded quickly, tapping his fingers together. "Yes, I could see him working on hinges. Or maybe chopsticks. Or maybe dog collars." He shrugged. "I certainly wouldn't trust him with a car door. He's no artist," he added in conclusion.

Dakota frowned. "Anything else?"

The second man cleared his throat. "There's probably two killers."

Dakota looked sharply at him. "What makes you say that?"

"Some of these bars," he said, pointing towards one of the images, "would be far too heavy for one person to lift. I would say that one is at least seven hundred pounds. I'd expect *three* people to lift it. Unless he had a forklift nearby."

Dakota shook her head. "No forklift. You're sure?"

Both men nodded adamantly.

Sylvia added, "Those *two* sisters were just killed. Maybe that's because there were *two* killers." She wrinkled her nose in disapproval. "It's like one of those horrible detective novels."

Dakota nodded in commiseration. "You're sure one person couldn't lift that?" she said, pointing at the metal piece in the image.

All three artisans nodded.

Dakota crossed her arms, frowning. Nothing in the MOs had suggested two killers. Was that how he was eluding them? How he was escalating so quickly?

The thought of multiple killers horrified her. If true, they were further behind than she could've first imagined.

She said, "Can you think of anyone like that? Any couples or friends or duos who would be involved in your scene? Artists, perhaps? Metalworkers?"

The two men in the sweaters shared a look, and, simultaneously, both said, "The creepy couple."

Sylvia rolled her eyes.

"Creepy couple?" Dakota asked.

The two men nodded adamantly "Yes," said Rowley. "We used to get parts and pieces from their junkyard, but I got *shot* at. Hear that? Shot at." He gave a disapproving shake of his head. The other man said, "They have these horrible dogs they allow to run wild over the place."

"A junkyard?"

Both men nodded.

"And who is this creepy couple?"

The woman snorted, "It's not a very polite thing to say, is it? Their real names are Johnny and Kimi Hendricks. They run a scrapyard not far from here. Part of the industrial zone—it saves a lot of the companies around here the trouble of having to ship it out towards West Chicago."

"Johnny and Kimi Hendricks," Dakota repeated. "How far is their yard from here?"

"A couple of miles," said the older woman. The men both nodded in agreement.

Dakota looked at them. "And what makes you bring up their name?"

The man with the mohawk snorted. "They would know how to weld and solder, but they've never been good. They've submitted to this convention before. We always have to tell them no. And they threatened us before—besides, they were very jealous when Sophie and Lauren's exhibit was accepted for the front stage." He pursed his lips and nodded once as if punctuating his point.

"Jealous how?"

"They accused Sophie of stealing their designs," said the old woman. "I was there myself as I sometimes help out with convention decisions. They demanded a meeting, accused the girls of intellectual theft. Called them plagiarists. Threatened them."

"Threatened them physically?"

The old woman paused, smacked her lips, and said, as clearly as she could, "If I remember correctly, they threatened to feed both women to their rottweilers." She nodded once.

Dakota felt a flicker of unease. "They physically threatened the victims?"

"Absolutely."

Dakota paused, considering this. They were local, which would tie them to the most recent crime scene. And if they had experience soldering and working with metal, that could connect them to the other crime scenes as well. She felt Marcus nudge her, and she glanced over. He was holding his phone so only she could see the screen.

She frowned, leaning in, and was immediately confronted by a mug shot

Johnny Hendricks. Marcus scrolled down, and Dakota's eyes widened at the black and white scrolling text.

Mr. Hendricks had a rap sheet as long as her arm. Assault, and two counts of domestic abuse. Marcus kept his tone calm, and low, but said, "Five assaults in the past, Dakota. All of them women in their twenties."

She frowned, glancing as he swiped through the file. An assault from ten years ago had been against a bartender. Another one had been against a woman in a grocery store. Still another had been against someone who'd come into his scrapyard without permission.

She shifted, staring at the picture of Johnny Hendricks.

"All right," she said slowly, "could you guys tell me precisely where his junkyard is located?"

She looked up. All three of them nodded and began to speak.

CHAPTER TWENTY ONE

Dakota double-checked she was buckled as Marcus sped through the streets, hastening away from the warehouse, through the industrial district. Generally, her partner enjoyed keeping speed limits, but now they zipped up the cracked and poorly maintained roads, sending up streams of dust beneath their tires. The same dust billowed over their windshield.

Ahead, she spotted a tall, rusted fence topped in sagging barbed wire. More than one location had a hole corroded through the fence. Long weeds jutted between gaps in the metal mesh, and beyond the overgrowth, she spotted piles of scrap and old appliances stacked in corridors next to junked vehicles and crushed jalopies.

Marcus slowed as they neared the gate to the junkyard, frowning and pointing through the windshield.

Dakota spotted it too. A blinking green light perched on top of an empty guardhouse. A camera pointed directly at them. The gate was shut, locked with a chain looped through the entrance and secured by a padlock.

Marcus frowned through the windshield. "Think we should hoof it?"

Dakota followed his gaze. She paused, then clicked the radio in the car. "Officer Lanzig?" she said.

A moment paused, then a staticky voice replied. "Roger."

She said, "This is Agent Steele, we're at that junkyard. Think you could send a couple units for backup?"

More static. "We expecting weapons?"

Dakota stared through the ominous, dilapidated barrier. "Don't know. One of the stall-tenders mentioned they were shot at for trespassing."

"Roger that. On our way. Might be a few."

"No problem," Dakota said.

She went quiet. The two of them sat in the quietly rumbling vehicle, the vibration of the engine only adding to Dakota's sense of stalled momentum. The killer was escalating—they didn't have time to just sit around. Marcus suddenly yawned, trying to cover his mouth. A second passed, then Dakota yawned.

"Sorry," Marcus said.

She waved away the apology. Her eyelids weighed heavy. Sleep had been in short supply over the last thirty-two hours. She closed her eyes against a headache.

Eyes still closed, she muttered, "They'll be here soon..."

"That's what he said."

"I mean... it couldn't hurt just to poke around a bit."

Marcus shot her a look, using his eyes, his head still forward. "Mhmm. The sooner we get this done... the sooner I can sleep."

As if they'd both reached the same conclusion simultaneously, they pushed their doors open and stepped out onto the dusty path in front of the locked junkyard gate.

Dakota approached the metal fence. She called out, "Hello? Is anyone in there?"

She frowned, looking one way then the other. More than one hole in the fence was large enough for both of them to squeeze through. She began to step towards the nearest opening, but then spotted something. She frowned, reaching out and testing the padlock.

It fell off.

Someone had snipped the lock but left it to look as if it were still securing the chain. A slow shiver crept up her spine. "Marcus," she murmured, nodding towards the chain.

He approached behind her, frowning as well. "That's odd," he murmured. "Wasn't... Wasn't there a lock like that back at the second crime scene?"

"The abandoned trainyard, yeah. I remember it. A padlock placed over the chain, but not actually secured."

She tentatively touched the rusted chain, the metal like sandpaper against her fingers. Dust that their car had churned up lingered on the air and she waved a hand beneath her nose to breathe easier. She tugged at the chain. It moved only an inch, but then the weight of the thing itself pulled it through the mesh. It rattled as it fell, each link bumping against the wire. It pooled on the ground like a coiling snake and then went suddenly still.

Undeterred, Dakota pushed out, opening the gate. It swung on greased hinges. At least these, she surmised, were well tended to.

"You coming?" she called over her shoulder.

Marcus hesitated, bleary-eyed and still yawning. He glanced over his shoulder down the road in the direction they'd come from. For now, no sign of approaching vehicles, no flash of lights. Hopefully their backup had the good sense to keep sirens off to avoid spooking their suspects.

Marcus finally relented, his shoulders sagging as he pushed through the gate as well, joining her on the dusty trail that sliced through the labyrinth of refuse and scrap.

"Just keep an eye out," she muttered. "No need to engage. We're just fact-finding."

Marcus shrugged. "This place is big. Almost fifteen acres. If we keep to the perimeter, we'll be fine."

Dakota nodded, pushing forward, her head on a swivel, keeping an eye on the large structures around here. As they moved forward, she could feel her focus narrowing, tunneling on the path ahead.

This had often been one of her best skills as a fighter—to push out the noise, the crowd, the flashing lights, the jeering, the taunts... All of it. Just to focus on one opponent. On the task at hand.

She inhaled through her nose and exhaled through her mouth as she moved through the dusty scrapyard. Johnny Hendricks's record had more than one count of unprovoked battery. She'd gone over more of it in the quick drive over.

The man was a rejected art school student. He worked in a junkyard that his father had owned and passed on after his death. To say the man's relationship towards the women in his life wasn't particularly favorable would've been putting it lightly.

Dakota's skin prickled as she thought back to one of the images that she'd seen in Hendricks's trial photo from nearly ten years ago. He'd bashed his first wife's head in with a pan. He'd tried to cut her with a knife. Not along the throat—but he'd been aiming for it judging by the barely healed scar along her collarbone that Dakota had seen.

As they moved along the path, cautiously, quietly, something suddenly appeared out of the corner of her eye.

A figure. Standing by the bumper of a trashed SUV.

Dakota jumped, hand darting to her hip. She hadn't heard a thing. But as she spun to face the assailant, she paused.

The figure was motionless. In fact, it was only shaped as a humanoid. The *thing* was streaked with dark grease. Part mannequin, part barbed wire. The wire wrapped around the mannequin's abdomen and curled down to the base.

Dakota stared, swallowing. "Marcus..."

"I see it," he murmured behind her. "Dakota let's stick back until—

”

But she hastened forward, approaching the horrible creation. The rusted barbed wire gouged into the statue's plastic features, cutting deep. Someone had crossed out the mannequin’s eyes with a black marker and then drawn a pentagram in the middle of the forehead.

Dakota stared, feeling a tingle along her skin. “Art,” she murmured. “I guess.”

Marcus grunted. “Art.”

As they reached the row of crushed cars, Dakota realized this wasn't the only sculpture of metal. There was weird art everywhere she looked. Some sitting on the hoods of the cars like ornaments. Others, more bizarre creations with many arms and jutting metal spikes, were placed like sentries along the rows.

It reminded her of trimmed hedges, except without any of the charm.

“Where's the main office?” she said, shooting a look towards her partner.

Clement gestured with an arm further down the same trail. “On Maps, it was against a back fence, near a dump site. I think we should hang back.”

Dakota paused, but then nodded, taking a step towards her partner and away from the strange metal and mannequin creations.

As she did, though, someone suddenly cleared their throat. “What do you two kids think you're doing here uninvited?”

This time, as she turned, she was certain she wouldn't be confronted by a statue.

She spotted him sitting in one of the rusted trucks. The vehicle had no wheels to speak of, or windshield, or mirrors or engine... It was mostly just a car frame placed on old, dead, yellow grass.

But a man was sitting inside, leaning back, his bare feet resting on the spot where a dashboard might have once gone but where a thin plank of wood now stretched. The bottoms of his feet were cracked and muddy, and he wore suspenders with no shirt. He was chewing on a cigarette butt and drinking from a tall glass of what looked like either iced tea or rum or a combination of both.

The man had mean eyes and grizzled hair. His salt and pepper stubble, instead of giving him a look of sophistication, only made him look sloppy in Dakota's view. One of the toenails on his left foot was nearly a quarter inch long, jutting past the dry skin of his big toe.

She grimaced at this, raising her hands in placation. “Apologies,” she called out. “Are you Johnny Hendricks?”

He watched her from beneath those hooded eyes. Instead of answering, he took a long sip from his iced tea. “So what if I am?” he asked. “I don't know you.”

Dakota raised her ID. “Agent Steele,” she said, icily, “FBI.”

The man's eyes darted from Dakota to Marcus. He smirked as he studied the big man. “I see they lettin' just all sorts in nowadays.” He chuckled, flashing a couple of missing teeth along with some rotten ones. “You FBI too, big guy?”

Marcus remained cool, raising his ID as well. “Agent Clement,” he said. “We'd like a word with you, Mr. Hendricks.”

“Now, now—see, I never said that was me.”

“Sir, we have your photograph. We know who you are. Where's your wife?”

“Walking the dogs. She’s around here somewhere.” He paused to flick his cigarette butt out the window then take another swig from his drink. He sighed, smacking his lips contentedly, then pushed out of the front seat of his stripped truck. His bare feet hit the dead grass in already trampled portions. “Gotta be careful of them screws,” he said, nodding knowingly and tapping a grimy finger to his long nose. He then plopped onto the hood of his car, glancing between the two of them and indicating Dakota with his tankard. Some of the liquid sloshed, spilling down the side and dripping to the ground.

“Well?” he said. “You got somethin' to ask—ask. I'm all ears.”

Dakota let out a faint little breath. She wasn't sure why, but something about the man's attitude was screaming *threat!* She couldn't see a weapon, though, nor did she spot anything that might be perceived as an ambush.

Sitting on his rusted truck, in the middle of a junkyard full of weird creations and quasi-artistic sculptures, Dakota supposed her misgivings might simply have been due to the backdrop of this particular encounter.

She tried to refocus, clearing her throat and saying, “Were you anywhere near the art show down in the industrial complex today?”

“Huh? What's that? Do I look like I'm there?”

“Just answer the question, sir.”

“No,” he said simply. He shrugged, his bare, bony shoulders lifting the straps of his overalls. He squinted, glancing up at the sun in the sky. “Still ongoing I reckon. Just started.”

“We heard that you were interested in attending. You're saying you never stopped by?"

He sneered suddenly, shaking his head. "Interested in—pshaw! Lies. Hogwash. I ain't interested in shit. They'd be so lucky. Look around you, lady—you're starin' at a modern-day Leonardo DiCaprio!"

Dakota hesitated. Marcus muttered, "I think you mean da Vinci."

"Him too!" hollered Johnny. He wagged a finger around in the sky and finally leveled it on the agents. "What's the reason for the questionin' folks? I don't got all day. Been busy."

"You look very busy," Dakota said slowly. As she spoke, her eyes moved past the man, sweeping the junkyard. She allowed her gaze to work as something of a metal detector, using the reaction of the junkyard owner as her gauge.

Every time she glanced off to the left trail, leading past a stack of busted dishwashers, he shifted uncomfortably, almost as if he wanted to stand in front of her and block her line of sight. She frowned, taking a step towards this area and pointing. "What's down here, sir?"

"Hey now!" he said, sharply, some of the teasing, jovial tone being replaced by a sharp bark. "You can't be here. You ain't got one of them—paper things. Whachoo call it?"

"Warrant?" Dakota guessed.

He nodded, pointing. "You ain't got a warrant. Stay where you are."

Dakota was ready to correct him on this point, but before she could, she heard the sound of clinking chains, slobbering, heavy panting. Then footsteps came as well. A few moments passed and a woman emerged at the end of this same path Dakota had been peering down, stepping from behind a shipping container. The woman strolled nonchalantly forward, leading two rottweilers on leashes. She wore shoes and a shirt, thankfully, but her clothing wasn't in a much better state than her husband's.

Dakota could almost smell the grease and WD-40 from here.

"Ah, there we are. How's it going hon?" Johnny called, waving at his approaching wife. "We got us some guests."

The woman was frowning as she drew nearer though, her eyes narrowed. If her husband's gaze could've been described as *mean,* hers was downright *nasty.* Dakota supposed in some cases opposites attracted. But more often than not, in her experience, birds of a feather flocked together.

And these two birds were not the sort to be intent on sharing their nest with strangers. Even federal strangers.

"Hey, you can't be here!" Mrs. Hendricks called, shaking one of her chains and picking up the pace. The two slobbering beasts leading her were panting, drooling but pausing every now and then long enough to shoot hungry glances in the agents' direction.

Marcus stepped back, one hand at his holster, another extended towards the hounds and their handler. "Stay back," he warned. "Stay back!"

Mr. Hendricks sneered, "Wachoo gonna do, suit? Shoot my dogs?"

Mrs. Hendricks's scowl—and seeming sense of hygiene—matched her husband's. She stalked forward, rattling the chains. "Come on now," she said. "You two ain't supposed to be trespassing."

"Ma'am," Dakota said, keeping her tone even, though adrenaline was now racing through her body. She could sense the impending threat drawing nearer. So far, no sign of a weapon on the two. The dogs, though, were baring teeth—clearly homeschooled pups without much fondness for strangers. "We're FBI," Dakota repeated. "I need you to stop coming towards us."

"You're trespassers!" the woman screeched. "Damn authoritarian pricks! Get off our land. Get out of here!"

"Ma'am—stop now!" Dakota warned.

"Stay back!" Marcus called.

But she was shaking her head. Her husband was egging her on with faint giggles while slapping a greasy hand against his leg. "You tell 'em, Kim," he was saying. "Go on you two, get!"

Dakota wanted to look over her shoulder to see if backup was on its way, but she didn't want to risk losing line of sight with the suspects. The strange, looming creations of metal and mannequin around them only fueled the uneasy atmosphere. No distant sound of sirens; though she'd asked them to keep the noise to a minimum. No flash of lights off the tall walls of junked metal either, though.

They were on their own. The couple was behaving aggressively. Over-aggressively. The sort of behavior two killers hoping to get away with murder might exhibit? Unwilling to go down without a fight?

Dakota saved her breath now, slowly lifting her weapon from her holster, but aiming it towards the ground.

Mrs. Hendricks noticed the motion. Her cruel eyes narrowed, her gaze piercing Dakota like some jackdaw. And then, she clicked her tongue. "Told you to leave," she muttered. "Have it your way. Beemo! Bambam! Go!" She reached down and unhooked the strained chains from the taut collars.

The rottweilers loosed snarls and barks and then, at twin pats from their owner, bolted forward in blurs of brown and black.

"Hey! Hey, don't you—" Marcus tried to shout, but too late.

Dakota had an angle on the first hound, her finger tensed on the trigger. But shooting another person's dog? Even scumbags like this? It was protocol, but Dakota had always had a soft spot for animals with sucky owners. So she kept her gun low and instead hurtled back, shouting at Marcus, "Get off the ground! Off the ground!"

Agent Clement hadn't even drawn his weapon. Briefly, Dakota wondered just how badly the shooting on the last case had affected her partner. She could still picture the blood streaking the warehouse floor. The woman bound in a chair, the faint tap of footsteps against cold concrete and the noxious odor of blood on still air.

Marcus liked people. Shooting someone went against the grain of his character. If there was one flaw he had as an investigator, it was that he was just too damn personable.

At her shout, though, the two of them moved towards the same source of protection. The rusted-out truck.

Mr. Hendricks's eyes widened, and he flung to the side, off the hood of the car, moving towards his perilous puppies.

The dogs ignored their owner, bolting right past him, jostling him enough, though, that more of his whiskey-tea sloshed out of his mug.

He was shouting after his hounds. "Get 'em boys! Go Bambam! Go!"

Dakota didn't have time to try and intervene with the man though. Things were escalating fast. No gunshots yet. Where was backup? Shit. She flung herself stumbling onto the rusted hood of Johnny's dilapidated truck. Marcus hit it a second later.

It wasn't like most vehicles. Normally, some bodyweight would have been absorbed by a faint bounce, the tires and shocks. But as this thing was missing its tires. And probably everything else; it instead felt like slamming into a brick wall.

Dakota cursed, scrambling up; Marcus had launched *over* the hood with his giant gait and landed on the roof of the truck.

The chains in Mrs. Hendricks's hand rattled where they dangled, loose and limp. The dogs snarled, teeth flashing as they both hit the front of the truck at the same time. Then came a horrible sound of unclipped claws scrambling against untreated metal.

Dakota rolled sharply, wincing where her arm scraped against the rough surface. Something cold seeped through her sleeve—spilled tea.

Slobber speckled her exposed ankle. Teeth scored across the rubber of her shoe. She shouted, kicking out—a shove-kick, sending one of the dogs flying back. Her sympathy for the curs didn't extend to the possibility of rabies.

"Told you two to get!" Hendricks crowed.

His wife was trying to tug his arm, though, dragging him back and whispering fiercely in his ear. Dakota could only pick out the occasional word over the sound of her own beating heart, her scrambling motions on the metal hull, and the hullabaloo of the rottweilers.

"...out of here..." she was saying. "More... up..."

Her husband muttered a few times, yanking his arm petulantly from her grip, but at last he seemed to relent. He allowed his wife to guide him hurriedly away from the dog and the agents, hastening down a row of old jalopies. More strange metal sculptures stared out with vacant eyes along the road that led away from the car. Then, the couple disappeared around the edge of a shipping container, vanishing.

Dakota's heart pounded as Marcus dragged her onto the roof next to him. The two of them pressed back-to-back, legs tucked up, huddled against each other and, momentarily, out of the reach of the hounds. The dogs hadn't yet realized if they reached the top of the hood, they could then make their way to the roof. Instead, they were now at the base of the left passenger-side door, both snarling, leaping, claws scraping against the metal doors before landing back on the weeds and yellow grass. They circled a couple of times, trying from different angles, still glaring and growling.

Dakota felt a flicker of frustration. Her gun was holstered again, and she was loathe to draw it, even to protect against the dogs. For now, they were safe. But if one of the hounds got near to mauling Marcus, she realized—with a sinking sensation—she wouldn't have a choice. She'd have to put it down.

Still, for the moment, it hadn't come to that.

Her heart pounded. The dogs scraped and scratched and slobbered.

And then, a new sound.

An engine. The grumble of an old, struggling vehicle. A second later, a small pieced-together jalopy emerged around the edge of the same shipping container. This car was moving *fast.* A cloud of black smoke spat up from the exhaust, trailing with the dirt on the air.

Mr. Hendricks was whooping and hollering, pumping a fist out of the window as they sped hastily past the stationary agents on their island of rust.

Mrs. Hendricks was driving, and didn't look towards Dakota, keeping her eyes fixed on the cramped road that led back out of the junkyard.

"Shit!" Dakota snapped.

She stared, glaring after the fleeing vehicle. They couldn't stay up here—the suspects would get away. She felt her stomach twist, turn. She gritted her teeth and then raised her weapon.

No choice. She had to do it. She aimed, then pulled the trigger.

CHAPTER TWENTY TWO

The gunshot rang in her ears with a loud *snap* like a firecracker. Her aim was true. One of the mannequins toppled with a loud *crash* slamming into a stack of washing machines. At the sound, the rottweilers turned sharply, still panting, still slobbering. Dakota shot another mannequin. This one toppled as well, ricocheting off the corrugated metal side of the shipping container. One of the mannequins' heads fell off, hitting the ground and rolling.

Bambam first spotted the head, turning faintly.

"Go on," Dakota muttered beneath her breath. "Come on—just go!"

She shot the mannequin head again, sending it rolling like a ball across the ground. "Nice aim," Marcus muttered.

Dakota shushed him, nudging him towards the edge of the car in the opposite direction of the beheaded mannequin.

Both the dogs were now facing the rolling white ball-shaped item. They shot frustrated looks back towards their prey perched on the top of the rusted truck. But now, the loud *bangs* from the gun were frightening them. While the playful tottering of the mannequin head was enticing.

It took them a few more seconds to make up their minds. Precious seconds in which the Hendricks were still speeding away in their junker vehicle. Instead of heading towards the road, though, they reached the gate and instead turned sharply to the *left* back into the junkyard, along a row of stacked cars. Dakota couldn't be sure why, but she supposed backup was possibly visible now on the horizon.

Still, there was likely more than one exit to this place.

Finally, as one of the forearms of a metal creation toppled and began rolling down a slope, the rottweilers turned and broke towards their new toys, scampering after the head and arm.

"Now!" Dakota hissed.

Marcus and Dakota shoved off the truck, hitting the ground softly and moving as quickly, but silently, as possible back up the road, towards the gate.

They both broke into a sprint. The dogs suddenly barked, and Dakota heard the sound of pursuing paws.

“The car!” she shouted. “Get to the car!” She could only hope she'd bought enough time by sending the dogs the other direction for those precious few seconds.

Marcus and Dakota sprinted down the hill, shoulder to shoulder, choking and coughing on the dust and exhaust lingering on the air. It smelled of diesel and cigarette smoke.

The dogs chased after them. The fifty-foot gap they'd managed to create rapidly closed. Far, far faster than Dakota would've first thought possible.

Thirty feet. Twenty.

The dogs covered the distance in a blur of brown and black. Ahead, past the gate, Dakota's eyes settled on their parked vehicle. The sound of keys jangled next to her where Marcus held them in one hand. She noticed his other hand kept pumping at his side but occasionally tapping against his holster as if assuring himself it was still there.

But for the moment, he was following her lead. Neither of them wanted to kill the dogs. And neither of them wanted to get mauled or let the Hendricks escape.

At a breakneck pace, the two of them sprinted towards the ajar gate and their motionless vehicle.

The dogs closed the distance—if they'd been well-fed or watered, at all, Dakota felt nearly certain they would've caught up. As it was, though, the hounds were already tired, lagging. But still, doggedly, they pursed.

Ten feet, five. The slobbering, the snarling was the ghoul at her heels. Dakota reached the gate, slipping through; Marcus followed a second later. The headlights flashed as he clicked the locks.

“Get in! Get in!” he shouted.

Dakota ripped her door open, and Marcus followed a second later. Bambam caught the edge of Dakota's sleeve, ripping at it, but coming away with fabric.

She flung herself into the car; Marcus did also.

The doors slammed in synchronization, and suddenly, the sounds from outside their stationary vehicle were muted. The panting, the barking, the growling faded to a muffled background noise. Now, the only sound was the heavy breathing and faint coughing inside the vehicle as the two agents tried to dislodge the dust from their throats.

“Shit,” Dakota said.

“Crap,” Marcus concurred.

They both heaved, leaning back in their seats. Dakota knew dogs didn't know how to work handles, but just in case, she pressed the lock to her door. In the mirror, behind them, about a mile up the road, she spotted flashing blue and red.

"Backup," she muttered.

Marcus nodded, letting out a wheezing breath. "Maybe we should've waited."

Dakota shook her head though, pointing at the cameras. "They would've seen us waiting. Might've let them grab a weapon, or bolt. We need to go after them, Clement. Each second wasted..."

Marcus sighed, his massive chest rising and falling beneath his unbuttoned suit top. The comic book shirt beneath was stained with sweat. He shook his head in frustration but then muttered, "I know... I know..." He slipped the keys into the ignition, started the car, and began to trundle back towards the gates just long enough to warn the hounds. The rottweilers backed away, still barking, but now very much a nuisance rather than a threat.

Marcus brought their car against the gate, bumping the metal further open until they were able to crawl through the entrance. Then, he turned sharply on the side road where the Hendricks had escaped. The dust was still swirling, lingering on the air.

"Think they're gone?" Marcus said.

Dakota just adamantly shook her head. "They spotted the cops and peeled off. Must be there's another way out of here."

Clement picked up the pace, flooring the pedal, hastening through the junkyard, moving along a maze of metal and scrap. More sculptures and metal creations leered down at them from along the side of the road, like some poorly constructed Halloween haunted house.

The attempts at depth or artistic expression only made Dakota's skin crawl. She couldn't shake the images of the very real victims these killers had left behind. The stall-tenders back at the convention had seemed certain. *Two* killers. It would've taken *two* people to lift such heavy metal bars. And now, their two suspects were out of sight.

Marcus reached the end of the large space, turning up the dirt path.

Dakota suddenly froze. "There!" she pointed sharply.

Marcus followed her indicating finger. His eyes suddenly widened as he spotted the source of their suspects' delay.

Another gate. This one locked. Mrs. Hendricks was still sitting in the driver's seat, pounding her hand against the horn in order to rush her husband. Johnny was busy trying to find the proper key, attempting to fit it into a padlock for the gate that led onto a long, dirt road heading in the opposite direction from the front entrance.

"Go!" Dakota shouted. "Go! Marcus!"

"I'm going!" he shouted back.

And he was. They zipped faster, faster along the road. Dakota bit her lip, feeling a surge of excitement. The two junkyard owners were shouting at each other now. Still struggling to find the proper key for the—

Johnny crowed, pumping a fist very much in the same way he had when leaving the agents to his hounds. The padlock came off. The chain rattled and he tossed it over his shoulder towards Marcus's vehicle. They were still about a hundred feet away. But closing the distance.

Johnny flung himself through the window as his wife nearly ran him over.

Dakota cursed in frustration. They were going to get away. The gate was open now. The backup wouldn't know about this off-grid road. Did it even lead back to a highway?

"Marcus, careful!" Dakota said suddenly.

Her eyes were fixed on a tall stack of precariously placed vehicles on the other side of the gate, about twenty paces *past* where Mr. and Mrs. Hendricks were picking up speed. This part of the junkyard extended past this second exit, closed off by fencing and wire. The tops of the jutting cars were visible over the barbed wire. Johnny was pumping his fist again.

Dakota cursed, shouted, "Steady!" Then, as Marcus gripped the wheel, she lowered her window, catching a mouthful of exhaust and dust. She leaned out the window, trying not to gag, aiming towards the stacked cars.

Her eyes were on a truck that still had its tires—somewhat inflated—halfway up the mountain of vehicular rejects.

She aimed, heart in her throat. Fired. Missed. Fired again. Hit.

One of the tires popped. The Hendricks had made it through their gate, and were navigating along the bumpy, jarring road ahead, slower than before, but still moving.

Marcus yelled in surprise.

"Watch out!" Dakota warned.

The popped tired on the precariously balanced truck wobbled. The four cars stacked on top of it also shook. Then, the truck slipped.

The vehicles perched upon it went the way of a Jenga tower.

They fell, crashing to the road in front of the fleeing getaway car.

A loud honk. A screech of tires. Then a screech of voices coming from the car ahead of them as the Hendricks' path was completely blocked by the toppled vehicles.

"Yes!" Dakota shouted, feeling her exhaustion, her weariness, lifted momentarily by pure elation. This time, she pumped her fist. Then, realizing what she was doing, she cleared her throat, sat straight-backed and muttered, "Good job!"

Marcus nodded, shooting her a wide-eyed look. "Wow. Good shot, Steele."

She smirked but hid it just as quickly.

They skidded to a halt, kicking up more dust. Their doors flung open again. This time, mercifully, not to the sound of baying rottweilers, but bawling junkyard owners. Johnny and his wife were screaming blame at each other. Their windows were open, but their bumper jammed against one of the toppled jalopies. They tried to back up to go around, but Marcus and Dakota were now sprinting forward, weapons raised.

She was tired of playing nice.

"Get out with your hands up!" Dakota bellowed. Even as she said it, she spotted another metal creation staring at her through the fence to her left. The mannequin's blank face gazed at her from beneath the front bumper of the truck she'd shot, its metallic and plastic form pressed to the wire mesh, with the lowest tangle of barbed wire gouged into its head.

She shivered, tearing her gaze away and fixating on the most immediate threats. "Get out!" she shouted along with Marcus. "Hands up! Now!"

Fingers jutted out windows, shaking and trembling.

"Don't shoot!" Johnny bellowed. "We was just playing. Don't shoot!"

"Hands! Hands!" Marcus's subwoofer of a voice boomed.

Mrs. Hendricks was leaning towards the glove compartment.

"Hands!" Dakota shouted as well. Their guns were fixated on Hendricks's wife now. Both of them circled, crouched, preparing to dive to safety. And then... a few moments passed, and Mrs. Hendricks let out a scornful sigh.

She finally, with painstakingly slow movements, raised her hands and pushed them out the window as well.

Dakota and Marcus rushed forward at controlled but rapid pace, their weapons unwavering, their eyes fixated on their targets.

“Get out of the car! Get out with your hands up!”

Dakota opened one side of the jalopy and Marcus flung open the other. The junkyard owners reluctantly exited their vehicle, grumbling and muttering. Johnny said, “Lucky shot.”

Dakota didn't care. She was already reaching for her handcuffs while the shirtless man in overalls ate a mouthful of dirt.

CHAPTER TWENTY THREE

The door opened and shut for the second time in as many minutes. Dakota listened to the sound of rapid footfalls squeaking against the tiles outside the interrogation room. "Sorry!" a voice called as the door shut.

She glanced back to see where a file had been placed inside the room just on the wall counter beneath the glass one-way mirror.

She watched as two police officers wrangled their suspects into their seats, cuffing them in place despite the spitting, clawing, and hurled abuse.

Mr. and Mrs. Hendricks were acting like a couple of stray cats being dipped into a bath for the first time. They fought tooth and nail, but at last, with a bit of help from Marcus, the two police officers were able to cuff them to the table. The sound of the chains around their ankles rattled as the suspects continued to strain at their bindings.

Dakota hadn't initially wanted the ankle chains, but after the first few attempts of getting the Hendricks up the stairs, she'd relented to the local PD's suggestions.

Now, Dakota was sitting across the long metal table, eyeing the two suspects. The police officers who'd helped escort them were both panting and sweating. One of them had a claw mark across his face where Mrs. Hendricks had scratched him. Another was massaging his ribs where he'd been elbowed by Johnny.

Both of them were shooting dirty looks towards the suspects, interspliced by occasional glances towards Dakota and Marcus as if making sure their services were no longer needed.

"We're fine," Dakota said, nodding in gratitude.

"Thank you," Marcus added, voicing Dakota's concealed sentiment.

She flashed a thumbs up, wincing as she did. She needed to remember to express her appreciation more in moments like these. Whenever Marcus did so, it seemed to garner fondness and respect from his peers and subordinates alike. The art of navigating human emotion, though, was still in the aspiration phase for Dakota.

Where she excelled, on the other hand, was studying people.

So she sat there, quietly, watching and listening as the two suspects continued to shout and hurl insults at Marcus and the two retreating cops. One of the cops grabbed the file on the counter beneath the window and placed it on the table in front of Dakota. The man muttered, "Good luck..." then, as he was leaving, added beneath his breath, "You're going to need it."

Dakota didn't disagree. But she didn't speak either. She waited for Marcus to rejoin her on their side of the table. Johnny, hands both cuffed, was flashing both birds at the same time. His lips seemed perpetually curled into a permanent sneer.

Dakota was ignoring most of this though. Both of them were leaning forward in their seats. Aggressive motions. But aggression was often camouflage. She'd fought more than one opponent in the ring who talked a big game up until the bout. Then, when the cage door slammed, and fists were raised, they'd suddenly cower and reveal their true colors.

There was nothing more honest than a cage fight, in her opinion. No more posturing, no bravado, no farce. At the end of the day, when a cage slammed shut, all that remained were two souls locked in combat. The mettle of either combatant was quickly revealed.

So she didn't mind, in that moment, the hissing, the cursing, the expended energy. Another thing she knew, when people were trying to get a rise, often the best approach was to simply let them gas themselves out.

Then, once they were tired and burnt out, she'd go in to glean what she wanted.

"You can't keep us here, bitch!" Johnny was shouting. "I know my rights! Hey—hey I'm talking to you."

"Look at her ear, Johnny," his wife sneered. "Ugly little lumpy ear. Probably has an ugly little lumpy brain."

"Yeah!" Johnny exclaimed. "Stupid fed!"

Dakota remained motionless, sitting at the table, weathering the storm. Marcus was scowling and looked ready to interject something, but he caught himself. He'd been partnered with her long enough to let Dakota move at her own pace. This, in her estimation, was just another reason they made such a great team.

Dakota kept watching. Flickers of fear flashed in their eyes. The aggressive postures were also leaning slightly *away* from each other. They presented a unified front, but this was only a show. The way they were acting, the way they were posturing, suggested all wasn't rosy in the Hendricks' love life.

So far, though, all they stood guilty of was lackluster hygiene and using their dogs to attack federal officers.

Finally, Dakota spoke. "I suppose you two know why you're here?"

At her words, a moment of quiet fell, as if the suspects couldn't quite believe they were finally being talked to. Hendricks rattled his chains, still flashing his middle fingers. His wife though, stared at Dakota with narrowed eyes and leaned back in contempt. "We don't know nothin'!" she declared.

Dakota just nodded. "You're here for the murders of Lauren and Sophie Astelay. We also need to speak with you about the murders of Caitlynn Jackson, Michelle Stanton, and Terin Kramer." She spoke slow, as if reading roll call. Her voice didn't falter, her tone didn't change. She finished speaking and only then did she look up, allowing silence to fill the ensuing space as she glanced between the two suspects, waiting patiently.

The first thing Dakota noticed: neither of them, for even a second, looked surprised. Mrs. Hendricks seemed to realize their reaction wasn't that of innocent parties and after the initial accusation and cold-eyed indifference, she tried to cover by gasping sharply as if in offense, but one look at Marcus and Dakota, and she abandoned this attempt with a snort.

Instead, she said, her eyes like a crocodile's, "We figured as much."

Dakota frowned. "Pardon?"

Johnny leaned in now, snorting. "We knew you'd try to peg this shit on us. We've been watchin' the news. We saw it comin'."

Dakota steepled her hands on the table, staring across. "I see," she murmured. "You knew we'd find you."

"No—hang on," Johnny snapped. "That's not what I said. I knew you'd come for *us.*" He snorted. "I mean shit, I know how it looks. I've got a rap sheet as long as my big ol'—"

"Shut up!" snapped his wife. "Don't tell 'em shit. We want a lawyer," she said, nodding adamantly and sealing her lips. "*Lawyer. Now!*"

Dakota frowned, glancing sidelong at Agent Clement. He said, "A public attorney is on her way, but it's going to take some time."

"Well then we ain't got nothin' else to say," snapped Mrs. Hendricks.

But Johnny's face had turned red at the interruption. He was now shooting narrow-eyed, angry looks towards his wife. He jutted his scraggly chin out petulantly and said, louder than she'd interrupted. "I was *saying*—I have a rap sheet, and we've got our artistic reputation around these parts." He said both parts with equal looks of pride.

"You do have a reputation among artists," Dakota said, "But I'm not sure it's the one you think. They seemed to be under the impression you held a grudge against Sophie and Lauren."

"Pshaw—see! That's why I knew you'd come. It's why we bolted. Hell, I didn't wanna come back to this sorta hell." He tried to indicate with his hands, but the cuffs looped through a metal circle in front of him went taut. In the end, he settled for pointing about the place with his chin.

Marcus cleared his throat, frowning and clarifying. "So you knew your grudge against the Astelay sisters would come to light. *That's* why you attacked two federal agents?"

"Didn't attack anything," snapped Johnny. "Bambam did. You look fine anyway. Those dogs are gentle as sheep."

Dakota wanted to snort but held back the gesture, remaining stoic. Still, she couldn't shake the image of those slobbering lips and flashing teeth. Gentle as sheep. Right.

She sighed. "So you agree," she said finally, "that it looks bad for you two. You live within two miles of the last crime scene. Your junkyard gives ample supplies for the metallic creations we've found with the victims—I know those were mentioned in the news. And as you yourself have said, you have a long record of violence against women."

"Lawyer!" Mrs. Hendricks snapped, pounding the table.

Marcus shrugged, pushing to his feet.

Dakota didn't get up just yet, though, frowning and glancing between the two. There was no glimpse of remorse. No glimpse of sympathy for the victims. Then again, she couldn't really blame them. She wasn't sure she could've conjured much sympathy if she was facing the same accusations.

But that was just it—they seemed almost disgusted by the charges. Multiple homicides. If anything, Johnny almost seemed proud of his arrest record. His wife was still glaring. Dakota thought back to what the stall-tenders from the convention had said. It would've taken *two* attackers to move some of those metal pieces into place for the devilish sculptures.

She just shook her head, Marcus standing next to her, his long shadow casting past her. "I'm sure I can put a good word in with the DA if you help me understand *why*." She waited patiently, still watching, ever-attentive, never allowing an opponent to lull her into a false sense of security.

But again, the Hendricks just sneered at her. The contempt they carried was palpable.

"Whatever, lady," snapped Johnny. "I knew you cops was gonna peg me for the death of those stealing sisters. The other stuff was good work," he added. "I saw some of them sculptures. Pretty nice if you ask me."

"Johnny!" his wife snapped. "Quiet!"

But he was still irritated and instead raised his voice, shouting over her. "No—hell, I mean it! I wish I'd have thought of it first actually."

"But you didn't?" Dakota said, frowning. "Is that what you're saying?"

"That's exactly it. What I've *been* saying," Johnny crowed. "I didn't kill them. Didn't think to do it. My loss. But whoever that artist is—he's a master. A da Vinci. A Van Gogh. All I got is respect for that fella—let me tell you."

Dakota let out a huffing sigh.

"Lawyer!" Mrs. Hendricks was shouting. "Lawyer! Lawyer! Lawyer!"

Marcus was tugging gently at Dakota's shoulder, trying to guide her to her feet. She finally allowed herself to be lifted from her chair. She was still frowning, her stomach still twisting in anxiety, her lack of sleep coming in waves. She held back a yawn as she stood next to Marcus, facing their two cuffed and shackled suspects.

She'd never experienced this before.

Johnny's lack of remorse, his callous indifference, his reckless comments were having the opposite effect she might have first assumed.

Was he guilty?

Or wasn't he?

She bit her lip, trying to piece it all together. It didn't really make sense.

Marcus was still trying to guide her away. "We're not going to get anything else," he murmured. "Leave it up to the DA."

She sighed, allowing him to slowly tug her towards the door. But at the same time, her heart was pounding rapidly; her tongue felt dry in her mouth. There was something almost soothing about Marcus's tone. Something nearly... congratulatory about the way he was patting her on the back, guiding her towards the door.

Dakota could still hear rapid movement outside their room. The shadows shifting beneath the gap under the door.

The cops in the precinct were also out in full force. They also seemed certain they'd managed to apprehend the proper killers. But now, standing there, occasionally glancing back at Mr. and Mrs. Hendricks, Dakota was growing less and less sure.

They just didn't take care of themselves. They weren't cautious people.

That much was obvious. The grease-stained clothing, the unkempt hair. Mr. Hendricks hadn't even been wearing a shirt when he'd first been arrested. His feet, bare and mud-stained and calloused. Even the junkyard they'd owned—sagging portions of fence, rusted segments of rail and missing barbed wire.

Everything in disarray. Everything haphazard.

Why did that matter?

Because, she thought to herself, *the killer, or killers, took care of the bodies.* She could still picture the victims' forms. Their skin unblemished, flaws hidden. Intentionally displayed in carefully crafted metal dioramas.

Everything had been meticulous, cautious, careful. Nothing like this couple. They didn't even take care of themselves.

As Marcus opened the door behind her, trying to guide her out before the lawyer arrived, she felt a sinking sensation in her stomach...

What if she'd missed it? Johnny Hendricks fit the bill nearly perfectly. Everything from his rap sheet to his personality screamed guilty. And now there he sat, with that simpering smirk, complementing a psychotic killer's creations like only a narcissist could.

But even still... Dakota wasn't convinced.

The door clicked shut behind her now where she stood in the hall. Marcus was still patting her on the back using the hand he'd guided her from the room with.

He was forced to turn and face Officer Lanzig who was waving a file and trying to get their attention. The two of them broke off into conversation, and Marcus stepped away from Dakota, nodding as he listened to the smaller cop.

Dakota, though, felt like a ship lost at sea, no mooring post in sight.

She stood in the busy hall, leaning against the wall, trying to make herself as small as possible as she ran over her choices.

Marcus was smiling now as he spoke to Officer Lanzig. There was a strange energy throughout the precinct. Everyone seemed on the edge, excited, certain that they'd caught the killers.

But Dakota wasn't so sure...

Still, no sense alarming anyone. The suspects *did* fit the bill. She had to admit that.

But at the same time...

What could it hurt to double-check? She only had one lead remaining—no harm, no foul to follow up on a train of thought she'd already bought a ticket for.

She exhaled softly, turned towards where Marcus was still in conversation, but then shook her head, thinking better of it—this was all probably nothing; she was probably just paranoid—and she turned, marching quickly away towards the break room to do some research.

CHAPTER TWENTY FOUR

"Probably nothing," Dakota muttered beneath her breath. "Probably... probably nothing." She couldn't sit, out of fear of dozing off, so instead she stood in the break room, fingers flying across the keyboard on her computer, her eyes glazed as she stared at the flickering blue screen, trying to track the information.

She checked. She doubled-checked. Then checked again.

Three options. St. Wesleys' church on President Ave. Leksian brothers' outpatient care. Or a public meet-up organized from one of the convention centers.

All of them advertised treatment for AA, SA, or NA. Any of the A's required by denizens of the area. All within walking distance of Michelle Stanton's trainyard tent.

Dakota hesitated, staring at the three phone numbers she'd managed to compile. Probably nothing. The others were probably right—the killers were in custody. Johnny had loosed his dogs on them. Had tried to run. His wife had been reaching for a weapon they found in the glovebox. Even now, cops were combing through the junkyard for any evidence of the crimes. The Hendricks had the motive, the means, and the opportunity. The personal connection with the Astelay sisters paled in comparison to Johnny's record where women were concerned. Violence against females seemed to be par for the course.

It made sense he'd escalated. They'd been expecting the FBI. They'd seen the connections themselves.

"Because they know they're guilty..." Dakota said, speaking the thought out loud. But it felt more as if she were simply trying it on for size. The words didn't quite fit. They felt close—she knew that much. But... but something was off.

Why had the bodies been kept so clean? Why had the crime scenes been pristine? Meticulous, cautious, careful.

None of that matched the suspects currently jawing with their assigned lawyer.

Dakota shook her head, returning her attention to the computer screen. She tapped her fingers against the desk and reached a conclusion. Just a little prying. That was all.

She dialed the first number, drumming her fingers against the edge of her laptop as she waited to connect.

***

The craftsman sat on the park bench, breadcrumbs between his fingers. He just couldn't stop smiling. He watched as a jogger passed and tipped his head, nodding after her. She was keeping in shape, forcing herself to do the difficult thing. Game recognized game after all.

He looked appreciatively after the jogger's form, tracing the lines, the shapes, the colors. The sorts of things only creatives ever really recognized. He sniffed and turned away, still tearing at breadcrumbs and occasionally tossing them onto the ground. A couple of pigeons had wandered close but were keeping a wary distance.

He wasn't sure if they'd seen what he'd done to the last one or could just smell the crushed bird behind the trashcan.

Sometimes, he just couldn't help himself.

There was something quite beautiful about the red of the crushed neck streaking those gray-purple feathers.

He tossed another breadcrumb onto the ground, cooing. At the same time, though, he kept an eye on the apartment door across the street.

He wasn't slowing down.

No—the FBI, the cops, his audience, were expecting him to slow.

But he'd pulled off the last piece without a hitch. Another *perfect* creation. And him? The perfect craftsman.

He rolled his shoulders, watching the door then glancing at his watch. She'd be out soon. She never missed a meeting, did she?

He admired that about her... But what he didn't admire?

The constant whining. The bellyaching and moaning. Oh poor me! I have no friends! Poor me! I'm so lonely.

He snorted in disgust. Some people just weren't meant to recover. Weren't meant to survive. He didn't have the patience to let her persist. For weeks now she'd been complaining about her life. About her job. About her friends.

She needed help.

His help.

And so he waited and watched, eyes on that simple green door at the base of the townhouse. He glanced at his watch again. A few more minutes. He'd timed her for nearly a month. Always sitting across the street, in the park. Feeding the pigeons. Snapping their necks when no one was watching.

And waiting patiently.

Tonight, though—as with all the others—he was ready.

It was Wednesday night, after all. She'd be leaving soon. Only two more minutes.

He smiled again, feeling a faint shiver of pleasure as he remembered the look on the Astelay sisters' faces. They'd thought they were such big shots. Such hot shit. But he knew their weaknesses. He knew they'd needed him. Just like they'd practically begged him to carry their load for them into the warehouse.

He was their guardian angel. They just didn't appreciate him yet. But soon, when they ascended, when he purged them and cleansed them and fixed them...

Then they'd understand.

A soft click across the street. He looked sharply up. The green door was slowly opening. A figure emerged on the steps.

His smile faded. His heart pounded. He wet his lips, excitement surging through him.

Lights. Camera...

He began to stalk across the park, towards the sidewalk, his eyes on the damsel in distress. The woman who desperately needed his help. She just didn't know it yet.

***

Dakota clicked through the links in her email, feeling her skin prickle as she downloaded the files. The Leksian outpatient group hadn't been willing to provide a roster. She had a request pending but it wasn't crucial to her next step. If any of the groups were *least* likely to provide access to someone like Ms. Stanton, it would have been a clinic with a high upfront payment.

No... no, the two rosters she'd managed to get, from the church and the meet-up, would have to do.

She waited as the files downloaded, and then quickly copied the two rosters into a single document. Her eyes darted across the information across the top tabs. She hid all the lists except the ones under *Wednesday.* And then, slowly, she began to scan the information, careful not to skip a single name.

Almost fifty names were on the combined rosters from the two support group facilitators. Dakota read and re-read each name, carefully. They weren't listed alphabetically, so she took her time, scanning. As she glanced down the list, she could feel her frustration mounting.

No names she recognized. Maybe Wednesday night wasn't the connection she thought it was...

She reached the halfway point, skipping over *Riley, Latisha.*

She sighed, pausing for a minute to rub at her sleep-deprived eyes. She yawned despite herself, covering her mouth and waiting a moment for this new wave of exhaustion to pass. She'd forgotten just how *hard* it could sometimes be to work for the FBI.

In the back of her mind, she could still hear Agent Carter's disapproving tone. Could still feel her sense of frustration when she'd been told that the old case files for the killer from three months ago were locked without express permission from her current supervisor.

But not only was she fighting for her reputation. For this favor to access the old files. But also for the victims—for those who needed someone to defend them... Just how others had so often defended her. Others like Marcus. Not just her partner... but a friend.

Hell... Maybe even her only friend.

Coach Little counted too. They'd both gone to bat for her.

And what about her curly-haired, handsome techie? She glanced towards her phone, resisting the urge to check for a text message from Mark. That would have to wait.

She refocused, glancing at the list again, reading slowly.

She paused. Nearly at the bottom of the list... *no,* at the *very* bottom of the list. The next name was for the instructor... The name had been added last because there was no phone number or address attached to it.

But a name she recognized. *Stanton, M.*

Dakota stared, feeling a prickle warm her cheeks. She let out a shaking sigh. Two names above *Stanton, M.,* she spotted something else.

Initials. L.A. She'd glossed over these at first, tired as she was. But now that she re-read them, she glanced towards the phone number listed. With shaking fingers, Dakota lifted her own phone and called the listed number.

It rang a few times. Then, a voice spoke on the other end. *You have reached the voicemail box of Lauren Astelay...*

LA. The most recent victim.

Lauren Astelay had also attended the same group as Michelle

Stanton. Had Sophie Astelay also been at the group?

Dakota felt her pulse racing now, her heart trying to reach her throat. Her excitement mounted as she re-read the names, just making sure her eyes weren't playing tricks.

But no. The second victim had been attending the same sobriety group as the fourth and fifth victims.

Also, on a Wednesday night. Caitlyn and Terin had attended a separate group at the convention center, but also Wednesday. All of the victims had been attending sobriety groups for various ills.

Dakota swallowed, feeling her throat parched all of a sudden.

This bastard was targeting people in recovery. She felt a jolt of fury at this, considering her own path. Undoubtedly, this monster might have targeted her too if given a chance. Dakota pressed her teeth together. But her anger was short-lived, supplanted once more by sheer excitement.

Now, she was growing less and less sure that the junkyard couple fit the bill. The attention to detail just wasn't there. Even their strange maquettes back at their scrap yard weren't similar enough to the ones at the crime scenes.

No... But that left a problem.

What had the artisans meant when they'd suggested some of the components in the crime scene sculptures would have required *two* people to lift them.

How would the killer possibly manage it?

Two people, just not the Hendricks?

Or maybe...

Dakota tapped her fingers on the edge of her laptop again. The artisans had seemed so sure there were two culprits. But what if they were wrong? Duo killers were rare. *Very* rare. Especially among narcissists who didn't tend to trust the same way duo-killers did. So if not *two*... What if there weren't two but one *very* strong person?

It fit, in a way. A bodybuilder or someone who worked out enough to be *that* powerful would be disciplined. Probably take care of themselves...

She tapped a finger to her lips, considering this angle.

On one hand, if she was wrong, and there really were two attackers, then she was already running behind.

She glanced back at the list of fifty, frowning. There was no way she could track down every potential victim—not in the short timeframe in which the killer was constantly acting. But on the other hand, a bodybuilder or a strongman attending a sobriety group would be easier to find.

They'd stick out like a sore thumb.

It wasn't perfect, but it was something. She bit her lip, considering her next move, but then nodded to herself, reaching a conclusion.

She pushed away from the table, turned hastily and moved quickly back out of the break room, down the hall, hurrying in search of Agent Clement to tell him what she'd found.

CHAPTER TWENTY FIVE

Dakota kept tugging at the big man until she'd pulled him through the door into the dark stairwell. As the door swung shut, it mercifully cut off the sound of chatter, of hurry and rush from down the hall and throughout the precinct. Above, she heard footsteps on the stairs, but they were heading up.

For the moment, she'd managed to secure a brief window of privacy.

"Marcus," she said, "I think I found something."

He glanced at where her hand gripped his wrist, then back up at her. He slowly reached up without speaking, took off his glasses, cleaned them on his sleeve and replaced them again. "I see."

She frowned. "I—wait, was that a pun?"

He blinked as if confused. She shook her head and continued. "Never mind. Look, Clement, I don't think we've got the right suspects."

He inhaled slowly, held the breath, and then exhaled. Again, he didn't say anything.

Dakota took this as permission to continue. "I've been running over the rosters from—"

"What rosters?"

"The ones from the sobriety groups. Remember?"

"Ah, yes..." Marcus looked ready to add more, but then held his tongue. He just waited quietly, letting her continue.

"Well," she said, "Guess what I found?"

Marcus frowned. "Second victim?"

"And the Astelay sisters, too!" Dakota declared. "They were both attending the same AA group at a local church."

Marcus crossed his arms, standing in the darkness of the stairwell. "Is it possible Mr. and Mrs. Hendricks were trawling those groups?"

Dakota hesitated, wincing. "Possible. Of course. We should ask them."

"They're not exactly being forthright."

"No," Dakota said with a sigh. "And that's where my concern is. They're not the most subtle people."

Marcus rubbed at his chin. "No, I suppose not."

"They're not cautious. Not careful. Do they look like the sorts that could've planned these murders? Executing them without a hitch?"

Marcus gave a long sigh but, in the end, just shrugged. "They fit."

"I know that. I know all of that. But... look, it's not going to cost us much."

"So what's the next step?"

Dakota held up her phone. "Calling the group coordinators and seeing if they have a physically strong person attending their groups."

Marcus blinked. "Come again?"

"Oh—right. Didn't mention that part. But I was thinking, maybe there *aren't* two killers, just—"

"One really strong one," Marcus murmured.

She nodded, patting him on the arm. "You're a big guy. There was nothing at those crime scenes I don't think you could've hefted around. At least for a bit."

Marcus shrugged modestly. "If you're right, then he would stand out in these groups."

"Exactly." She trailed off, feeling a jolt of nerves. "So... you in? I can call the church if you wanna call the meetup."

Marcus pressed his lips together, but then let out a long, huffing sigh. She could see him weighing their options. She could see his reluctance to concede. Clearly, he wasn't convinced. She felt a pang of guilt, remembering the last time she'd made a call Marcus had disagreed with. A girl had died. A killer had escaped.

A sudden flash of pain jolted through her belly. In that moment, part of her wanted to take it all back. To just play it safe.

But she wouldn't have been able to do that. Not really, not without turning herself inside-out. All she could do was make the best call. If she got into her head over it, there'd be no end to second-guessing herself.

Still, the slow disquiet of unease whittled at her soul.

At last, though, Marcus relented with a sigh. "Fine," he said. "I'll call the meetup. We're looking for a bodybuilder?"

"Or anything similar," Dakota said excitedly. She scrolled to the open webpage on her phone, raising it so Marcus could see the phone number as he fished his own device out.

He entered the number and, simultaneously, the two of them placed their calls. Both turned away from each other, briefly, shoulder to shoulder in the dark recesses of the stairwell. Dakota listened as her dial tone rang, attempting to connect.

After a few moments, a voice said, "Hello, this is St. Mark's."

Dakota hesitated, swallowing. Churches brought to mind her childhood along with images of Sunday clothing and combed hair. Attempting to look like all the things she had never felt. She experienced a sudden unease, thinking back to her estranged relationship with her father.

All of it faded a second later as she forced herself to keep a professional tone. "This is Agent Dakota Steele with the FBI. I have some questions about the sobriety group you're running."

"Oh my. I'm sorry... Umm, just as far as—"

"I can give you my badge number if you'd like. You can look it up."

"Er, well... You know what—no, that's fine. I'm not sure what I can tell you, though."

Dakota said, "I called earlier about getting rosters. I think I spoke to a receptionist."

"Yes. I was told."

"You're the coordinator for the group that's listed?"

"Father Duncan. I help lead the groups. It's this Wednesday night. Were you planning on attending?"

Dakota wrinkled her nose, feeling oddly offended at the question. "No, thank you," she said stiffly. "I was wondering if there was someone in your Wednesday group that fits a specific description."

In the background, she could hear Marcus speaking on the phone as well. She tried to focus on her own conversation.

"What do you mean?"

"We're looking for a man. A very large, strong man. He would be a bodybuilder, or a particularly sizable person."

"And he attends tonight's group?"

Dakota said, "Yes. Or at least he would've in the past. How long have you been coordinating?"

"For a few years now. And actually, it's a funny thing, I wouldn't have thought I'd recognize a description over the phone, but there is Benjamin."

Dakota perked up. "Benjamin?"

"I'm afraid I don't have a last name. He's been coming for about a year now. He hasn't attended for a couple of weeks. But, that description, of course brings to mind Benjamin. He's a very large and very muscled man. Did he do something?"

Dakota could feel her fingers tapping against the back of her phone.

"He hasn't attended in two weeks?"

"Well, no. But funnily, we actually get RSVPs for the group. Just so I can know how many people to expect. Refreshments and that sort of thing. It helps keep costs down, so we don't order too much."

"Of course," Dakota said, hiding her impatience.

"Anyway. I bring that up just to say, tonight, Benjamin responded. He said he was going to be here."

"He did?" Dakota skin prickled.

"Yes. If you'd like to meet him, he should be here tonight."

"What time is the meeting?" Dakota said firmly.

She was only half listening, though, as her skin turned from a prickle to a buzz. There was a man who fit the description in a Wednesday night group where three of the victims had been attending. A large, muscled man who could lift the metal contraptions.

And he was going to be there tonight.

Dakota was already moving towards the door, listening intensely to the information as she hastened to the parking lot.

CHAPTER TWENTY SIX

Their vehicle squealed and hopped the curb, leaving rubber on the asphalt as the doors sprang open. Dakota and Marcus pushed hastily out of the car, facing the small corner church. St. Mark's resembled the side of town it occupied. Somewhat run-down, with more than one boarded-up window. It looked more like an office building than anything. And judging by the few cars in the parking lot, most of the attendees walked or took the bus.

Dakota glanced hastily at her watch, hissing sharply through her teeth. Her feet hit the pavement, and the scent of lingering cigarette smoke wafted on the air from a back door behind the church. A janitor's yellow mop bucket sat propping the door open.

Dakota marched up the concrete steps to the main door. Despite the setting of concrete and asphalt, the church door itself was a wooden thing with cheap but pleasant stained glass. Dakota pushed through with Marcus close behind.

A cork board with a large arrow pinned to it directed them down a set of stairs.

The two of them marched shoulder to shoulder, taking the steps two at a time, curling down the stairs and descending into the basement. Dakota's heart pounded in rhythm with their footsteps. Ahead, down a hall lined by water fountains and empty rooms filled with chairs, she heard the sound of voices. A second of pause, then faint sobbing. She scowled, hastening towards two large, beige double doors. Marcus on one, Dakota on the other, the agents pushed into the room beyond.

A small circle of people sat in chairs facing towards the center. With a quick count, Dakota determined there were only fifteen people currently in attendance. As she noticed this, she also endeavored to spot Benjamin. But there was no sign of the man she'd described over the phone. A few of the figures in the cheap chairs were large, but not in a muscled sort of way.

Currently, one such participant was sobbing into his sleeve, his shoulders shaking. Figures on either side of him patted his back in commiseration, whispering comforting words as they did. Some of the other group members looked uncomfortably away. While others just stared at their hands, lost in their own thoughts. One of the figures sitting in the group was a man with wispy hair and angled eyebrows. He perked up as the agents approached. He arose from his chair, shooting back an apologetic look towards the others and hastened forward, moving quietly and lightly on his feet as if worried he meet disturb the others who were gathered.

"Hello!" he said merrily as he drew near, his eyes twinkling with an excited energy. "Were you the person I was speaking on the phone with?" he said, eyes narrowing in on Dakota.

She nodded once. "Father Duncan?" Even the first word made her wince. *Father* anything would've made her cringe.

But if he noticed her discomfort, he didn't show it. Instead, he just smiled congenially and reached out a hand in greeting. He shook Dakota's then Marcus's hands vigorously and gestured towards the group behind him. A few of the members were glancing in the direction of the three figures by the door, but mostly they seemed absorbed in their own business.

"We're in the middle of a session but... you were here for Benjamin, right? No last name given."

"That's the one. I don't see anyone who—"

"I'm afraid he didn't show up."

Dakota frowned. "I see... Can you think of any reason he might have skipped?"

"I didn't tell him you were asking for him, if that's what you're implying." Those arched eyebrows rose like twin peaks on his forehead. His fingers pressed to his chest, indicating himself.

Dakota sighed, glancing around the group. More eyes were darting in her direction, some of them dry, but others red-ringed. She noticed a couple of empty chairs. Her eyes skipped to a concessions table by a small, wooden stage. On the table, she spotted water bottles. Nearly twenty of them. She frowned, glancing towards the chairs again. Father Duncan, on the phone, had mentioned he liked getting a head count for his meetings, so he knew how many people to order for.

She pointed at the empty chairs. "Missing more than just this Ben guy?"

He blinked, clearing his throat and adjusting his button-up shirt. He didn't wear a collar or a black robe or anything, not that Dakota knew exactly what to expect in a group like this. The man just said, "A few actually. Benjamin missed. Mrs. Givens is out sick."

"Mrs. Givens? How old is she?"

The priest frowned at the question but covered quickly and answered. “Hmm—I'd say she's in her sixties. Is that relevant? What is this about, Agent Steele?”

Dakota was impressed he remembered her name from the phone call, but she shook her head. “Never mind, forget about Mrs. Givens.” Too old, she thought to herself. Out loud, though, she said, “Is anyone else absent?”

“I—yes...” he said slowly, frowning as he did. His eyes darted between Marcus and Dakota as if gauging them. At last. he just sighed and shrugged. “Two others. Ms. Peacock and Ms. Wolf.”

Dakota stared. “Young women?”

“Y-yes... I suppose a bit younger than you. Why?”

Dakota could feel her adrenaline rising. Two women in a similar age range to the previous victims were missing along with Big Ben. “Is there any benefit to RSVPing the roster?” she said. “Any reason Benjamin might have?”

“I can't think of any. It just adds you to the email chain to vote on what snacks you want in the group.” He nodded towards the water bottle table and small bags of pretzels in a wicker basket. “I can't see why—”

But Dakota was starting to feel the prickle on her arms spread now. No sign of Big Ben in the group, but the killer was escalating at an alarming rate. Anyone could be the next victim. He chose people from Wednesday night sobriety groups, for whatever reason. And now two younger women who'd RSVPed were missing. And this last comment by Father Duncan provided a fresh illumination. “So he would've seen who *else* responded to the email?” she said. “That's the benefit of replying?”

“I suppose so. But why would—”

“Ms. Peacock and Ms. Wolf, you don't happen to have their addresses, do you?”

The priest hesitated. Marcus flashed his badge preemptively eliciting a sigh from the man of the cloth. “I—they both happen to attend church here. Not as regularly as I might like,” he smiled in what he seemed to think was a jovial way, but then said, “But I have their information for our meal train. We like to support members in our community who—”

“Right—thank you. We need those addresses!” Dakota said urgently.

“I—do you have a warrant?” he said.

"It's for their own well-being," Marcus replied, "Sir. We have reason to believe they might be in danger. We need to send units to check on them. Now."

The priest's face went pale. He stammered a couple of times, but then murmured a quick prayer, crossing himself before turning on his heel and hastening towards an office door in the back of the room. "One moment!" he called over his shoulder towards the group. He added a glance towards Dakota and held up a finger, indicating the same sentiment.

He hastened with clapping footsteps into the office, disappearing from view.

Dakota's foot tapped a tattoo into the floor. She could feel her skin prickling, her anxiety mounting. What were the odds that this Benjamin fellow, who fit their description perfectly, would RSVP but not show up on the same day that two women didn't? But which one was he targeting?

She pressed her teeth tightly together, staring towards the office door and willing the priest to hurry. She began moving towards it, but paused, something catching her eye out of the corner.

She was barely even looking, but for some reason she stopped to read a single sentence written in red marker and cramped handwriting on a whiteboard. The group members were now chatting with each other, a bit louder. A couple were helping themselves to the pretzels and waters.

But Dakota just stared at the whiteboard. A simple phrase. Not a particularly unpredictable one. But for some reason it stopped her in her tracks.

The first step to sobriety, it read, *is forgiving yourself.*

A couple of the letters were smudged. And she was pretty certain the last word was misspelled. But as she stared at the sentence, she felt something twist in her stomach. Her own longing... her own burden to bear. She'd never come to a group like this. Two weeks sober currently... But then again, was she really?

She felt a flicker of doubt, of unease. For a moment she even forgot why they'd come. She knew the reason she chased the bad guys so doggedly. Knew why she would put herself in harm's way to catch a killer. Marcus so often concerned himself with the victims, but Dakota focused on catching the bad guys. It meant a lot to her to see survivors, to know she'd helped those who would otherwise have been victimized. But what gave a rush—an unhealthy rush, perhaps, was the idea of putting evil people behind bars.

She stared at the whiteboard again, re-reading the simple sentence. It rattled around in her brain, whispering in her ear, etching itself across her mind's eye. She pressed her teeth tightly together, ripping her gaze away from the whiteboard. She was fine. She could do this on her own. She'd done it for two weeks now, hadn't she?

Besides, now wasn't the time for existential questions.

She heard the clap of footsteps and felt something akin to relief as Father Duncan reemerged from the office, hastening towards the two agents with a faint frown on his face.

"I—I have the addresses," he said slowly, "but I tried calling. Neither of them is picking up."

Dakota gritted her teeth. "You're sure? Neither?"

"It's very possible they didn't recognize my number. A lot of the members in this group are here for... particular reasons. They tend to avoid calls from unknown numbers as a boundary. Often they delete toxic influences from their lives and don't want to risk giving access."

"So if we call they won't pick up?"

Father Duncan shook his head sadly. "Another thing, here..." He extended two slips of paper. "This is Cameron Wolf and this is Alissa Peacock. They live on opposite sides of town. Alissa takes a taxi to get here, and Ms. Wolf is one of our few members that drives."

Dakota could feel her stomach sinking. Marcus accepted the notes with a gracious nod. He handed one of the addresses to Dakota while taking one himself. Dakota bit her lower lip, considering and then said, "I'm afraid I have one last favor to ask, Father Duncan. I need to borrow your car."

The priest, to his credit, didn't hesitate. "I suppose you could just make me give it," he said. "But I won't protest. If they're in danger, then it's yours. Just, if possible, bring it back with a full tank. I have little league tomorrow in Geneva."

Dakota accepted the keys gratefully, and was already moving, Marcus falling into step behind her. The two of them hastened back out of the room, towards the stone steps again. Dakota could feel her heart pounding as she said, "You take Alissa. I'll take Cameron."

Marcus nodded but was already on his phone. He let out a faint breath after a moment as the two of them emerged from the church. "No one's answering," he said. "It won't even let me leave a voicemail."

"Shit," Dakota said. "Fine—call for backup. Get them to meet us there. Take care, Clement. Go fast. We might already be too late!"

She broke into a sprint, pressing the key fob and watching for a car to flash. Marcus raced towards the haphazardly parked sedan. The two of them moved with the urgency the situation demanded.

Already, Dakota could picture the horrible murder scenes of the last five victims. They'd been a step behind so far. She refused to fail again.

Lights flashed from a run-down, rusted hatchback, but it would have to do. There was no time to wait for another car. She glanced at the address, hastily typing it into her GPS as she simultaneously tried to start the car and then nearly dropped her phone in her haste.

She cursed, slamming a hand against the dash and forcing herself to slow down. The GPS chirped its first instruction as the engine rattled to life. A small little crucifix on beads dangled in the window and the car smelled of a cheap gas-station air freshener. She rolled down the windows as she squealed out of the parking lot. Marcus was already turning one way and she sped through a stop sign, hastening in the exact opposite direction.

CHAPTER TWENTY SEVEN

The priest's car moved far slower than Dakota would've liked. But she floored the pedal anyway as she took the turn off the highway into the small northwest Chicago subdivision where quaint homes and even quainter parks and bike paths lined the recently swept streets. The GPS directed Dakota onto a side street, and she picked up the speed, her hands gripping the steering wheel.

Ahead, she spotted Cameron Wolf's address a second later, the numbers on the door frame standing out like gold in the failing light, illuminated by the glow from inside the porch. Save the porch light, the house was completely dark. Dakota's teeth pressed tightly as she veered sharply up the driveway, slammed on the brakes and burst onto the sidewalk, sprinting up the steps. As she ran, she thought she felt something vibrate in her pocket. She ripped her phone out, glancing down. No news yet from Marcus, just a warning she was running low on battery.

She clicked the screen off and reached the front door of Cameron Wolf's home. She pressed the doorbell twice and knocked loudly. "FBI!" she shouted. "Ms. Wolf? Is anyone home!" She knocked again, more firmly. No response.

She stood there, skin buzzing, heart pounding. All she wanted to do now was kick the door down or break through a window. But she forced herself to remain calm. Focused. No signs of breaking and entry as she scanned the doors and the windows. She knocked again, pounding a fist against the frame beneath the porch lights.

As she breathed heavily, adrenaline lacing her system, her mind zipped back to the last time she'd just missed a killer. She'd split up with Marcus then too. A woman had died, and Dakota had spiraled into depression.

Now, sleep-deprived, exhaustion weighing heavy, she refused to let it happen again. She pounded louder, knocking frantically, ringing the bell. Still nothing.

She sprinted down the steps, glancing along the side of the house. No broken windows. No—*there.* One of the windows was slightly ajar.

Shit. She had to make a call. Backup was still on its way. What if, at that very moment, inside the house, in the dark, the killer was crouched, waiting for her to leave?

Dakota cursed, sprinting towards the open window now. “Ms. Wolf!” she screamed. Normally, Dakota prided herself on keeping her emotions in check. But now, she felt like a live wire, everything going haywire. Her skin buzzed in anticipation as she flung herself towards the open window and dragged herself through, slithering. At least this way she wasn't breaking down a door and alerting the killer.

She landed with a faint *thump* inside a living room. A dark TV was positioned on a wall above a small bookshelf stacked with cooking books. She glanced around, in the dark. No sign of a struggle. One of the chairs, though, was off kilter. She pushed to her feet, moving with soft footsteps towards the door, her hand moving towards her weapon.

Then, suddenly, the lights flicked on.

She froze, eyes bugging.

Two figures stood in the doorway staring at her with rage in their eyes.

In horror, she thought briefly that she'd missed it. There *were* two killers. But then, she calmed enough to take the new arrivals in. A woman and a man. The woman was wearing a bathrobe and curlers. The man had a towel wrapped around his waist. Both were soaking wet, dripping water and suds on the floor. Both smelled of roses and chamomile. Further down the hall, through an open door, Dakota thought she heard the dulcet tones of romantic music playing over the sound of a humming shower.

“Ms... Ms... Wolf?” Dakota said, wincing as she stared at the woman in the bathrobe. Dark patches of moisture had soaked through the robe. Soap bubbles were popping at the woman's feet where she stood, dripping and gaping, and staring in fury.

“Who are you!” Ms. Wolf screamed. “Jeremy! Jeremy call the police!”

“Hang on, hang on!” Dakota said urgently, raising one hand in placation, the other whipping out her ID. “I am the police! FBI! Agent Steele.”

The expressions of the two figures shifted from angry to scared in a heartbeat.

“What happened?” the man said, nearly dropping his towel and showing far more leg than Dakota was comfortable with. She looked determinedly up and away.

“I'm very sorry, Ms. Wolf. We had reason to believe you might be in danger. Why did you skip your group tonight?"

The man glanced at the woman. "Group?"

Ms. Wolf's cheeks reddened, and she shrugged. "What group?" she said, glaring daggers at Dakota.

Dakota hesitated, then quickly covered. She didn't like lying herself—tried to avoid it out of sheer habit, even for a righteous cause. But a little bit of deception often was part and parcel with the job. So she said, "Father Duncan was mentioning how helpful you've been with your service. That's all."

The woman let out a faint little sigh, relaxing a bit. The man was still glancing quizzically at her. Cameron Wolf said, "I—I had a date tonight..." she shot a look towards the man in the towel, then blushed. "I—we only just... It's not what it..." Suddenly, she seemed to realize how it all must have looked. Dakota pinpointed the exact moment when the self-consciousness fell across Ms. Wolf's expression. "Don't tell Duncan," she said quickly.

"Who's Duncan?" the man demanded.

"My priest," she replied quickly. "He's not—I don't..." She looked miserable now.

Dakota, wincing, hands raised began backing away. She'd already embarrassed herself. So she aimed to leave through the window a second time. It wasn't like she was going to be able to much improve the impression she was making. "Sorry," she said quickly. "I'm very sorry for interrupting. Ms. Wolf, if anyone comes to your door, please make sure you know them before letting them in."

"What's this about?" the woman demanded.

Dakota just shook her head. "Lock your windows. And doors. Stay inside for tonight, please. Just to be safe."

The woman and her boyfriend both looked flabbergasted, frozen in place. The faint sound of breathing and tapping water droplets replaced the scraping of the window as Dakota opened it further. She realized how silly it must seem now, climbing through a window a second time. But there was no time to awkwardly ask to use the door. No time to delay.

She'd chosen the wrong house. The killer wasn't here. It certainly wasn't the small man with Ms. Wolf. No—she was at the wrong place. Unless... he could always come later. Shit. She had to make a choice... She'd have to make sure a couple of cops sat on the house. Just in case.

Dakota ignored the shouted questions from inside, simply lobbed back , "Lock the doors and windows!" Then she sprinted up the side of the house back towards her idling vehicle.

Marcus was alone, heading towards the remaining potential victim. If the killer was in wait, Dakota was too far to do anything about it.

She redoubled her pace, throwing herself into the front seat. She hit the gas and the tires whirred, squealing as they tore out of the driveway and back onto the street.

CHAPTER TWENTY EIGHT

Agent Marcus Clement could feel his skin prickling as he knocked on the door a second time. He waited politely, patiently, listening for a response. He'd made good time to Ms. Peacock's address, but he knew time was of the essence.

Marcus glanced down at his phone, double-checking he hadn't received a message from Dakota.

Nothing. His partner was likely still en route.

He sighed, glancing back towards the parked police vehicle and the small garden hedge circling the home. This was a nicer area of town, and he'd spotted more than one mansion lining the suburban street. He'd even spotted a few children playing in their front yards on pink bikes or with foam baseball bats as he'd driven past.

A neighborhood where bad things didn't happen. Certainly not the sort of neighborhood he'd grown up in—at least not at first. Not until he'd been taken in by his uncle and aunt. Dakota didn't know how he'd grown up. He'd never really shared it. In his mind, he thought it was because she'd never brought it up.

But neither had he.

Afterwards, after the bad phase—his first ten years—everything had become good again. His aunt and uncle had been upper middle-class. They'd even adopted him, called him their own son. They hadn't been able to have children themselves, so they had taken Marcus in.

After that, he'd had everything a boy could ask for. And often he tried to forget those first ten years. The neighborhood he'd been from. What had happened to his parents...

What he'd seen.

He let out a faint little sigh, adjusting his shoulders.

"Hello!" he called, knocking louder. "Ms. Peacock? FBI! My name is Agent Clement!"

He tried to put a bit of good humor to his tone. Sometimes, neighborhoods like this didn't respond well to people who looked like him. He'd long since given up on resenting them for it. Sometimes, it twinged when he had to put on an extra smile just to walk into a supermarket without getting followed by one of the clerks. Other times, like now, he couldn't help but feel past experiences colored current ones.

He didn't like assuming the worst of people. Most everyone, in his experience, had a lot to like about them. But there were always a few who threatened to ruin it for the others.

He sighed, knocking on the door of the quaint two-story. He put a little bit more emphasis into his entreaties this time.

And as he did, the door swung inwards, scraping across something on the other side. He frowned, bending down and examining a bent carpet, folded in on itself, helping to wedge the door in place.

"Hello?" he said, a bit louder, his voice quavering. He frowned, shooting a look over his shoulder, scanning the street. No car in the driveway. No car parked on the sidewalk. But also, there was an expansive two-car garage.

He turned his attention back to the yawning door, pushing it open a bit further, a faint prickle now crawling up his skin.

The carpet resisted his motions for a moment, holding the base of the door in place, but he managed to shove past it. The extra momentum sent the door slamming into the wall with a loud *thump.*

A coat tumbled from a hook behind the door, falling across his arm. In the past, Marcus might have jumped, but he'd been on the job too long to be scared by something like a falling jacket.

Besides, the jacket—now on the ground—didn't look much out of place in the ransacked home.

He stared, his eyes as wide as saucers as he scanned the space, his gaze darting about. A dining room table had toppled. A TV lay smashed against the ground. Kitchen knives scattered across the hallway which led to a tiled kitchen.

"What in the world," he murmured to himself.

Briefly, Agent Clement froze in place, his mind flitting back to another time, a past life. A similar scene of havoc. Then, they hadn't had nearly as much stuff in the house to destroy. But it had looked like a ransacking, on a smaller scale.

Marcus shook his head, heart in his throat. "Ms. Peacock?" he shouted into the house now, already pulling his phone to call for backup. "Hello? Anyone?"

His other hand moved towards his holstered weapon. He took a step over the carpet, sliding along the wall, moving carefully, cautiously. His ears were perked, and he listened for any sign of movement.

And that's when he heard it. A faint thumping sound coming from a closet in the middle of the hall. Was that a cry for help?

He stared, eyes wide. Was something seeping beneath the door? He slowed his breathing, steadying himself. This was the part of the job he hated most. This was why he needed Dakota around. When it came to people, interactions, psychology, or memory, he was happy to go toe to toe with anyone. But in moments like these, when someone was undoubtedly hurt, he mostly just felt a slow chill.

He approached the door carefully. For the moment, no sign of blood. The liquid he'd spotted on the ground was just water from a small bowl that had been knocked over.

More thumping against the door now that he approached. Another moan.

No... Not a moan.

He opened the door quickly, gun in hand.

A shape darted between his legs, bounding across the room and flinging itself up the stairs. Marcus jerked back, stumbling but catching himself a second later. He stood motionless, panting, staring after the fleeing feline. Not a moan. A meow.

He adjusted his spectacles and then heard the phone connect.

Before he spoke, he gave one last cursory glance around the place. No movement. No motion. No blood. He lowered his weapon.

She wasn't here.

A second later, this same thought gave him a flash of terror.

She wasn't *here.*

So then where the hell was she?

***

The craftsman whistled breezily as he strolled up the public street, nodding and smiling occasionally to anyone who caught his eye. In one hand, he gripped his rucksack. The same backpack he used whenever he jogged around the city—it helped him keep his legs in shape. Plus, he liked the added challenge.

Over his shoulder, he carried the carpet.

A special carpet—he'd made it himself. Padded with foam and cushion to perfectly maintain the muse. No blood either—she was unconscious this time. Normally, he liked completing his jobs on site. But this time around it hadn't been advisable.

His friend from the Wednesday night group had called. The silly little woman had a crush on him, had been trying to get him to ask her out for months. As if he'd ever stoop so low. Would a god dine with a mortal?

He snorted, hefting the rolled-up carpet and marching gamely along.

The woman in question who'd mentioned the cops had stopped by hadn't had any clue what she was aiding him in. He never would've told her. He didn't believe in coworkers. He would share his glory with no one, that much was certain.

But at least it had warned him. He even thought he'd passed one of the cops nearly ten minutes ago. But now he walked on, the thick carpet draped past his equally massive form. No one suspected what he kept *inside* his folded fabric.

No, no—they wouldn't guess. They never did. Hiding in plain sight—that's how he thought of it.

He smiled as he whistled and continued marching along.

"Need a hand?" a voice said.

He paused, glancing towards a squat man with peach fuzz and a sunburnt neck. The man looked like he probably smelled. He was smiling and pointing towards the carpet.

The craftsman just scowled.

"No. Don't be silly."

He continued walking. But the squat man fell into step next to him. "Damn, dude, you have a girl's voice. Got some of that t-ball, huh? Steroids? I mean—haha, who the hell am I kidding? Course you're on 'roids. Look at ya. Look man, I can help you carry that. You got a fiver or something? I just lost my wallet last wee—"

The craftsman turned, staring down his nose at the incessant, nagging *thing.* "Go away," he said simply. His voice went deeper now, his eyes narrowing. His shadow spread across the irritant.

"I—okay, dude. Don't gotta take a tone. I get it. I get it. Fine! Sheesh." He backed away and the craftsman heard him muttering expletives as he moved off, marching down the sidewalk, past other pedestrians.

None of them suspected a thing. They never did.

A few admired his physique, as was warranted. Others stepped out of his way, while still others pretended like they didn't see him. All of it stark jealousy. Even their frowns were praise in his mind.

He smiled now, feeling the comforting weight draped over his shoulder, and he picked up the pace, still whistling merrily.

CHAPTER TWENTY NINE

The priest's car protested such speed with whines and shudders, occasionally jerking to the left or right with no warning and forcing Dakota to correct or risk veering into oncoming traffic. She cursed as the car jolted again. As she sped on the tollway, though, setting speed records in the 15mph zone of the I-pass booth, her phone began to ring.

One hand gripped the rattling and jolting wheel, the other navigated for her device, clicking it on a second later. The car, of course, didn't have Bluetooth. So she was forced to raise the phone. But this way, the vehicle kept threatening to jerk to the side, so she hit the speaker button, tucked the phone inside her shirt, resting it on her shoulder, and shouted, "Yes?"

"Dakota," Marcus's voice came hurried and faint.

She strained to hear him over the whine of her car. "Marcus—killer wasn't at Wolf's. I'm on my way to you now—"

"She's not here! Dakota, can you hear me?"

"I can hear you. What do you mean she's not there?"

"Someone was. But they're gone."

Dakota felt an icy prickle at these words. "Is there sign of a B and E?"

"I'll say—the place is ransacked, Steele. A complete mess. One of the chairs was turned to splinters." Marcus's voice was tense, and she could hear the sound of panting as if he were hoofing it somewhere while giving her the update.

"Where are you headed now?" Dakota asked.

A pause, a long gasp then a deep inhale as if Marcus were trying to gather himself. Then as Dakota careened around a semi-truck, Agent Clement's voice came over the phone again. She missed the first couple of words thanks to the screeching horn of the truck behind her but managed to piece together the meaning regardless. "—too late. I've already put out an APB. Locals are combing the house for clues, but there's nothing. No sign."

Dakota growled, her hands tensed on the steering wheel, her heart leaping in her chest in a desperate attempt to escape what felt like a tightening cavern. Again, she remembered the last time she'd split up with Marcus.

"No, no, no," she murmured to herself. She refused to lose another. She couldn't. *Wouldn't.*

Now, she reduced her speed, forcing her mind to calm. She couldn't think clearly when she allowed herself to get too emotionally invested. But at this point that ship had sailed. If she didn't think of something fast, another body would be on her conscious. She could feel the familiar tug and whisper of promises that came with inebriation. It started in her stomach and moved up her chest like an ache. It felt almost like anxiety, but deeper and more painful.

She shook her head, growling. Part of her remembered the words written on that whiteboard back in the church basement. The first step to recovery... Forgiveness was a tall ask. Doing it in community was difficult. Dakota preferred acting on her own—she could control the variables that way.

Now, she was quite literally white knuckling it. At least, the jalopy was under her control for the moment. She racked her brain, trying to think through her options. Any clue she might have missed. Anything she might have overlooked.

She wrinkled her nose, moving through traffic...

It wasn't much, and perhaps it only came to mind due to the miserable effort driving this junker. But she thought back to the neighbors' camera footage outside the Kramer residence. The third victim's driveway had been empty. No car on the street either. No sign of an approaching vehicle.

Dakota wrinkled her nose, thinking how they'd located St. Mark's recovery group in the first place. Walking distance.

That's how the second victim had managed to reach the group every night. *Walking* distance.

She bit her lip.

What if the killer's car didn't show up on the neighbor's door cam because he didn't drive himself... What if...

She felt a flash of inspiration and pulled sharply to the side of the road, her heart pounding a million miles per minute.

"Marcus! Marcus, I think I might—hang on, okay, stay on the line! I'm looking something up!"

She hit her blinks, the front headlight scraping against the concrete barrier on the side of the highway as she came to a complete stop. More vehicles blared their horns as they surged past, but Dakota completely ignored them.

The car hadn't been on the door cam footage...

Walking distance. What if the killer was also walking to the Wednesday night groups?

It wasn't much to go on, but she had to try *something.* And she had another clue. A clue the killer had practically thrown in their face. On its own a data point wasn't very useful, but combined?

Walking distance and welding. *Fabricating,* as some of the professionals had called it.

She searched her web browser, her fingers shaking from how tightly she'd been gripping the steering wheel, her hands moving quickly. She pressed her teeth against her lower lip in a nervous gesture, scrolling through the results.

The line was still connected with her partner, and she heard Marcus trying to get her attention again. "One second," Dakota was murmuring. "Give me a second."

"Dakota!" Marcus pressed. "What is it?"

She ignored him briefly, reading through all the results for fabricator shops within walking distance of the church group. She wished Duncan had the killer's address—but the man clearly hadn't been a church member. Just a predator in the weeds. As for her working theory, the killer could easily have taken taxis or trains, paying in cash when needed. But if she was right—if he didn't have a car, then what if he was just *walking* everywhere? Or, perhaps, running. Some of the locations would've taken hours by foot. But the killer was some sort of health nut, wasn't he? That's what Father Duncan had described. Maybe he was quite literally running to his murder spots.

But what about the metal sculptures? Suddenly she realized... The abandoned trainyard, the scrapyard just by the Kramers' house. The killer wasn't bringing his wares with him. He was finding them on location. So where was he taking his newest victim? Had he knocked her out, carrying her under the cover of night? Was he threatening her with some sort of weapon?

Perhaps he'd even heard Marcus coming and had been forced to improvise...

Dakota stared at the search results. Two welding shops within a walking distance of St. Mark's. One of them, though, according to the webpage had odd closing hours. Specifically on Wednesday night.

"Marcus!" Dakota shouted. "I think I may have found him. I'm texting you an address. Meet me there!"

Even as she said it, copy-pasting the link to send to her partner,

Dakota could feel her anxiety digging deep into her chest. There were no guarantees. What if the killer's version of walking distance was further than Dakota's?

For the kills, it seemed so... But for the Wednesday night group? There was something comforting about keeping recovery close to home... Dakota knew this firsthand. It was a gut call. No guarantees. She could feel herself wobbling, standing out on a loose wire over a sheer drop.

But she had to do *something.* Besides, the odd hours at the fabricator's shop on Wednesday fit the timeframe, didn't it? Dakota cursed, veering back into traffic, blinkers flashing, and speeding towards the exit ramp to return to the city.

She would reach the shop ahead of Marcus. Backup would take some time—they'd already sent their assigned units to the wrong addresses. Dakota cursed, lifting her phone to call the coordinating officer back at headquarters. They might as well get the help of some local beat cops just in case.

But Dakota was only a few minutes away now. If she arrived first, she'd have to be prepared for the worst.

She felt her stomach sink as she made her final phone call. The last thing she wanted was to stumble into a room to find another dead woman she'd been too slow to save.

"Come on!" she shouted as she veered off the highway, curving along the exit. "Come on!"

Her phone connected to the officer coordinating their assigned task force. At the same time, the GPS chirped, *in two miles, exit left.*

Dakota felt as if the world were closing in. They were out of time. The killer had his next victim, and all they had to go on was her own tenuous call. A life was in the balance, and Dakota wasn't even sure if she was heading in the right direction.

CHAPTER THIRTY

Dakota pulled sharply onto the side-street behind the fabricator's shop. No parking out front. Not much at all out front, in fact, in this part of the city. The shop looked something like a jeweler's, with barred windows, reinforced and bulletproof. The front door itself had two layers, with a second cage door just inside blocking anyone who made it through the glass.

Dakota left the car doors open as she pressed her hands against the glass, smudging it and peering into the dark office. The shop didn't have a sign. Didn't have hours posted. Didn't look much like a shop at all. Either it operated purely by word of mouth, or it wasn't intended to be visited by customers.

Dakota couldn't make out much. Night around her only served to further darken the streets, the alley, the reflections of the windows.

For a moment she considered knocking on the door, shouting for attention. But something told her this would be a mistake. If the killer really was in there, no sense in alerting him.

She glanced around desperately, searching for some way in. As she stared towards the bulletproof, double door system, she paused, frowning.

There, a dark spot on the ground.

She dropped to a knee, reaching down and touching it. Blood streaked across the tile.

Her face chilled as blood drained from her cheeks. She tried the door handle. No luck. Tried pushing against it. No give. She took a step and kicked with a loud grunt.

Nothing. The door was made to withstand bullets—her foot and shoulder would only break against it. She glanced at her phone. Cops and Marcus were still on the way but minutes behind her.

Judging by the blood on the ground, their victim wouldn't have minutes. She couldn't go through the bottom floor windows or door... but what if...

She let out a faint huff of air. "Sorry Duncan," she muttered.

She turned on her heel and raced back towards the idling car in the alley. She backed out with a squeal of tires, slammed on the brakes, paused and offered up a little prayer, inspired by the cross dangling beneath the mirror.

"Holy shit," she muttered. No one was watching. This side of the street at night didn't receive traffic. Good thing for what she was about to—

She slammed on the gas, aiming for the glass window. Bullets were one thing. But a speeding vehicle aimed with full force?

The hood of the car crumpled on impact. The glass didn't shatter so much as *bend* in, splintering white but remaining one giant sheet.

Dakota jolted forward, her head ricocheting off the steering wheel. She groaned, groggy, wincing and touching at her forehead, testing for blood. Dazed, black spots dancing across her vision, she felt like she might throw up. Dakota took a second, inhaling the odor of smoke and burnt rubber.

At last, after she gathered her wits, grateful to still be conscious, she unbuckled, pushed groggily out of the front seat and stumbled onto the sidewalk to witness the damage.

The blacked-out display window of the fabricator shop was bent in on the side. Some sort of protective, sticky sheet kept the glass together, preventing it from falling in pieces. Dakota pushed with her foot, bending the rubber-like window in. Then, inhaling and cursing her luck, Dakota sidled, facing the wall to avoid carving her face on any residue of glass, into the shop beyond.

It was dark inside. Dakota stood in the gloom, listening for any sounds, any voices.

What she heard weren't bloodcurdling screams, though, but faint, tinkling music coming from further in.

Around her, she spotted strange machines, benches, tables with clamps and tools she didn't recognize. There were thick saw blades and drills and scraps and pieces of metal. Buckets of bolts and springs and old, used nuts and washers.

She stared around the space, sniffing as she detected a strong odor of grease. The music was what caught her attention, though. A faint hum coming from up a flight of stairs.

She approached the stairs tentatively, still rubbing at her bruised head. The anxiety in her chest was at an all-time high. Hand on her holster, she took the stairs slowly. She paused halfway up, glancing towards the smashed front window. No sign of red and blue lights. No sound of sirens.

Marcus wasn't here yet either.

She was alone—when hunting demons, isolation made it nearly impossible. But she didn't have a choice. Ms. Peacock was counting on her.

...if she was still alive.

Dakota felt a faint chill and she began moving up the stairs again, her one hand tight on her weapon, her other glazing the metal rail curling towards the second floor.

She emerged to the sound of cellos and violins reaching some sort of crescendo. Instead of work equipment, up here... things were far stranger.

Metal sculptures lined the walls or dangled from the ceiling or stood sentry along the floor. There were creations that resembled suits of armor, or others that looked like angels in flight, hanging by chains from the rafters. Bigger creations looked like dragons with open maws, while smaller ones like little train cars stacked on top of each other.

Amidst the sculptures and metallic pieces of quasi-art, Dakota spotted fitness machines. The normal treadmills and exercise bikes somehow seemed even more out of place in this loft than the metal sculptures did. There were barbells and dumbbells and bikes and ellipticals.

It was as if someone had packed an entire gym in the upstairs. All the machines looked well used and worn, the rubber on one treadmill stained so dark with sweat that it almost looked as if the material were two different colors.

Dakota took a hesitant step into the expansive, high-ceilinged loft.

And then she spotted movement.

Dakota stared, at first not quite believing her eyes. It was just another sculpture... it had to be. It was too large to possibly be...

But then the hunched figure began to turn slowly. He wasn't wearing a shirt, his muscles rippling as he pushed to his feet. A faint hissing sound was coming from his direction, and Dakota's gun was now fully raised, pointing towards the man. As his eyes settled on her, he didn't look startled at all. As if he'd heard her arrive but didn't even care. "Hands where I can see them!" she shouted. "FBI! FBI! Hands up!"

But as she shouted, the man just stared at her. A faint bluish light hissed at his side, and Dakota realized he was holding a live blowtorch. But even this was nothing compared to the sheer shock of the man's size.

He would've dwarfed even Marcus. The figure had to be nearly seven feet tall, with muscles the size of bowling balls. And there, at his feet, Dakota spotted the missing woman. She lay unconscious on the ground, hands splayed out, an ugly gash over her forehead. For the moment, she was breathing—evident by the slight oscillation of her chest.

But thick metal bars were holding her to the floor, looped through the ground like crochet wickets. The giant's foot was as long as the woman's forearm. Dakota shouted again, more an incoherent sound than any useful instruction. The man was staring straight at her now, a faint flicker of a smile creasing his lips. He looked her dead in the eyes, tilting his head slowly, the motions of his figure keeping rhythm with the symphony playing from unseen speakers hidden in the room.

"Hello there," the big man said. He had a surprisingly high-pitched, almost lisping voice. A tongue darted out, tending to a cracked lower lip. His smile turned to a smirk, and he didn't move at first.

"I said get down! Drop the blowtorch!" Dakota yelled.

The man sighed, muttering, "It's *not* a blowtorch."

But then, instead of listening, he stepped over the unconscious woman, dropping to a sudden gargoyle's crouch behind her. He was still impossibly larger than the small female, but now Dakota risked shooting the woman by accident.

She tried to sidestep, but the man moved with her, keeping his victim between them. He leered over the body like some feline predator, his motions slick and smooth, his muscles rippling, his body tensed like a coiled spring.

"Get away from her! Hands where I can see them."

But the man was humming now, along with the cello music, swaying a bit, his eyes closed. There was something almost erotic about the motions. At last, he gave a faint shake of his head. "I don't think so," he whispered.

And then he began to lift the blowtorch, extending it towards his unconscious victim.

CHAPTER THIRTY ONE

Dakota let loose a yowl like a wounded animal, taking two sprinting steps to the side for another angle. But the man followed the motion. His blowtorch still spewed jet blue fire on the air. Small trails of heat vapor wafted up from the nozzle. The woman on the ground, trapped beneath one of the bent metal wickets groaned now, trying to shift. Her leg caught on the loop of metal soldered to the floor.

The big man seemed calm, completely unconcerned. Dakota was beginning to hyperventilate but caught herself. The physical training of cage fighting often helped regulate her emotions in high stress situations. She forced herself to breathe, forced herself to focus on the killer. The woman was struggling to rise, only further serving to block Dakota's line of fire.

So she reached a decision: she lowered her weapon sharply, pointing it at the floor. "You don't have to do this," she said, speaking mostly just to stall for time.

The big man frowned at her, clicking his tongue and wagging the hot flame beneath his nose as if it were a finger. In that high-pitched voice of his, he murmured, "Don't have to? I want to... I'm here to help." He shushed the moaning woman, putting an actual finger to her lips. The digit was nearly the size of a small banana.

Dakota cleared her throat, making a sound if only to draw the killer's attention away from his victim again. "You're here to help?" she said slowly. So he was loony tunes. Great. The crazy ones were often the hardest to talk down. One could never predict their choices.

The man smiled, bobbing his head a single time. He used the finger pressed to the victim's lips to shove her rising head back against the cold floor. "Stay there," he whispered to her in a gentle, tender tone. "I'll cleanse you. I promise. It won't take long."

The woman's eyes were fluttering—she was still caught somewhere between awake and unconscious. The big man's blowtorch was moving far too close to her head, though, for Dakota's comfort. "I don't think she wants your help!" she said, trying to appeal on the victim's behalf. Her gun was still clutched tightly in her fist. If she had to, she'd take the shot—even if it meant risking the victim. She couldn't just sit by and watch him torture her.

But now he was frowning. His attention had once again diverted towards Dakota. “Want? It has nothing to do with *want,* little lady.” He wagged his massive head and patted himself on the chest. Never had Dakota seen such a self-congratulatory gesture before, complete with puffed sternum and haughty eyes.

“I did it for myself. But these things? They're stuck. Wasting away. I'm the only one to purge them. Without me...” he clicked his tongue. “They'll die...” He whispered this last part, his face twisting into a grotesque mask before settling back to haughty rest.

“Stuck how? You're hurting her—you realize that?”

“Purity takes pain!” he spat, slamming the base of his blowtorch against the floor. “Gold is refined only in fire! I refine them. I do what they can't do for themselves!”

“Is that what you did for Caitlynn Jackson? What about Michelle Stanton? Or Teri—”

“Their old names!” he snapped. “I've named them now. They're my creations after all.”

“You're insane.” Perhaps not the most insightful comment, but Dakota felt as if it were worth pointing out.

He giggled, swaying his head again as the music changed. More fiddle and flute now than cello. But he refocused. “I'm free! Don't you see me? Look at me. Have you seen such a specimen? I built this. I did, up here. I was once like them. A dirty little, rotten...” His face twisted as if he were sucking on a lemon. He whispered this last word, “...addict. Do you know this one?” he said, patting the cheek of the moaning woman. “Hmm? No—then perhaps you ought to just leave. Unless...” Suddenly he stared at her as if seeing Dakota in a new light. “Unless you've come for my help too...”

Dakota was struggling to keep track of the madman's ravings. Madman or not, he was an *enormous* issue. But he was also smart. Every time she side-stepped, he would follow, keeping the victim between them. One of his hands always hovered by her head, too, as if preparing to lift her in case Dakota raised and fired.

For all his talk of helping, he was clearly willing to use the half-conscious woman as a human shield.

“Look,” Dakota said, slowly. “I haven't seen anything as large as you. Not off a basketball court at least. Very impressive. How about you let me come closer and I can get a better look at you?” She winced, certain the ploy was obvious.

His snort of contempt initially suggested he'd reached the same conclusion. But then, he snapped, “If you can't appreciate what you see from there, it won't matter how close you are. Are you blind, little human woman? Hmm?”

“I'll put my gun down,” she said, desperately searching for the words to get the reaction she needed. “I'll put it down and then you can put the blowtorch down. How about it? That way I can see you better...”

The big man suddenly grinned at the suggestion. “I see... A sort of... competition?” he asked. “I like competitions. The one in the trainyard was quite slow. I allowed her to try to outrun me. The first one—the pill-addict tried to out-climb me. The last two...” he tutted. “Tried to out-*create* me. But you... you think you can compete with me?”

Dakota wasn't sure what direction this was going now, but at least he wasn't torturing or killing anyone. “What sort of competition?”

“A foot race?” he paused, then frowned. “No... no, not that. I've done that. I won.” He bit his lip, then his eyes widened in delight. “Oh—I know! What about a bit of a tussle, hmm?” He wagged his head excitedly, his features dimpling like a schoolboy's. “Yes—yes I like that. A tussle. You lower your weapon—I'll lower my paintbrush and we can see which of us is the true piece of craftsmanship.”

Dakota shifted uncomfortably. A fight against a man that size? She was asking for it. But there were still no sirens. No sound of approaching cops. She was still on her own and the woman on the ground didn't have anyone else to help her.

The man was already leaning towards her again with his weapon.

At last, Dakota cursed. “Fine!” she said. “Fine—fine I'll do it. Here, see, I'm putting it down.” She heard the sound of the metal weapon striking the floor, it mirrored the noise of her heart dropping to her toes.

With shaky footsteps, she stepped away from the gun.

The man smiled now, flicking something on his torch and the light died. With a faint, shuddering breath, he exhaled deeply. Then, he gently, with caressing fingers, lowered the blowtorch to the ground by the woman's head.

Dakota took another step away from her gun.

And then the man's smirk turned into a sneer. With a bounding leap, he crossed half the distance between them, launching over the unconscious woman. And he sprinted straight at her, howling as he approached, fingers extended like talons.

Dakota only had a split second to reach a decision. Too long to try to reach the gun, raise it, find the trigger, fire.

No. Split-second, she stood her ground, waited until he was on her, his shadow swallowing her like a whale gulping a minnow.

And then she darted to the side, hands up, protecting her face, knees slightly bent, pushing off the back heel. Not perfect form, but good enough. She avoided the monster and he stumbled back.

It took him a second to realize he'd missed her. He howled, turning sharply and glaring at her in the dark. Dakota bounced on the balls of her feet, hands bunched into fists, swaying slightly. She'd never faced an opponent this big, especially not one with such dire consequences.

She knew, even as a trained cage-fighter, the bigger they were the harder it was to *make* them fall.

David vs. Goliath was a nice story. But ninety-nine times out of a hundred, she'd seen how those battles went. And the scorecards were never on the shepherd's side. For a second, the giant paced, like a lion—the two of them squared off in the room full of metal-makings, reminding Dakota once again of the cage.

His eyes darted up, glancing at her injured forehead where she could still feel blood causing her hair to stick to her skin. His nose wrinkled as he stared at the wound in her skin. "Yuck," he whispered.

And then he came again, shouting as he did, fist flying. Again, Dakota backpedaled. Avoid, dodge, hit when she saw an opening—and most of all: *never* let him get his hands on her. If he took it to the floor, it would be over before it even started.

He howled as he missed again, his fist slamming into a full suit of armor, sending it clattering to the ground in many pieces. Dakota tripped over another sculpture. The big man had to duck one of the flying angels. He lunged towards her, trying to wrap his arms around her waist, but she avoided this also.

Just keep distance... Just keep—shit!

He had her leg—having lunged again. This time she'd avoided the punch, but he'd gone low. No more dodging this—he'd lowered his head. She brought a knee up *sharp.* Crack! Straight to the chin.

Anyone else, it would've wobbled them. Maybe even knocked them down.

But the big man didn't even seem to feel it, almost as if she'd tried to pummel granite. He did, however, loosen his grip on her leg and she was able to scoot back.

Now, he was coming slower, breathing heavily, sweat drenching his brow, trickling down. In this light, he looked almost ghoulish, with almost no body fat to speak of, his tendons like cords, his muscles like hunks of meat. They moved when he did, like a small army of shapes moving to the music around them.

Dakota stumbled into another statue, nearly tripping, but using the thing to shove off and keep her distance.

The big man was no longer breathing heavily. When she realized this, her stomach sank. She'd been hoping that by getting him to come after her, the smaller fighter, he'd gas himself. But by the looks of things, he was only just getting started.

He clicked his tongue, shaking his head at her. "Nowhere left to run," he whispered.

And even as he said it, her head tapped against the wall. Her shoulders scraped a window. *Shit.* He was right. She tried to sidestep to the left. He lunged. She dodged to the right, but he'd been expecting this and caught her around the waist.

And suddenly, he was on her.

The man towered over her—his shoulders three times as thick as hers. He wrapped his gorilla-sized fingers around her, squeezing her waist tight. She felt her ribs protest, aching just from the pressure of his damn fingers.

She tried to kick and connected perfectly to his stomach. But he didn't even seem to feel it. He tutted at her. "See," he whispered. Even his breath smelled like mint. "I told you I was special."

And then he tackled her to the ground. Four hundred pounds of mass landing on a buck ten. Dakota was strong, trained. She worked on her physique. But she was no match for the sheer size of the monster.

It felt like being caught in an avalanche or crushed by a tsunami. The air burst from her lungs immediately. Her insides clenched—her gut twisting in that *sick-to-the-stomach* feeling from the sheer size of the killer.

He was trying to smother her with sheer weight. Dakota just needed an inch of space. Some room to move. Ju-jitsu had been one of her strongest weapons—mobile, acrobatic motions on the ground. The big man couldn't be punched. But everyone had to breathe.

Herself included. She couldn't move. Couldn't shout. Couldn't do *anything.* She just needed an inch. Just a little room to move. Just...

Black spots across her eyes. Head pounding. No air. Lungs aching. Kidneys, stomach, liver all protesting, mashed against each other. Everything in protest, ache and pain.

But this wasn't a cage fight. She didn't have to fight fair. So she didn't.

She brought her knee up as hard as she could. But there was just no room to gain momentum. So instead of slamming her knee between his legs, she barely grazed him.

So instead, she bit his nipple as hard as she could.

It was the only thing she had left. *Yuck.* That's what he'd said when he'd seen the blood on her forehead. She remembered the pristine condition of the murder victims' bodies. He'd *hated* bloodying them or causing damage to their skin. All she could think—*hope*—in that moment was that he had a similar aversion to piercing his own person.

She chomped down on his chest, biting as hard as she could, covered by an avalanche of meat and muscle and bone.

Her teeth sank into skin. She tasted blood.

And the man above her howled in pain. He jerked back, trying to tug away, but this only caused ripping. He screamed and reached down, wrapping his fingers around her throat. One squeeze, and she felt nearly certain he'd crush her larynx—not that she knew what a larynx was. Marcus would, undoubtedly.

But all she'd needed was an inch of space. Some ability to just *move.* And the moment he jerked back in pain, she seized her opportunity.

Using her left hand, she pushed her body along the ground, shifting enough to jut one leg out. With a hand, she grabbed a finger, twisting and bending it. Something cracked. He screamed again. With her loose leg, she hooked around his back, pulling him into her guard. Then, twisting the broken, mangled finger, blood trickling from his chest against hers, she pulled him to the right.

He screamed in pain.

Big as he was, fingers cracked easy. The motion of twisting him gave her the ability to now hook her arm on his left side. A foot and an arm. That's all she needed.

He was still trying to strangle her.

But by taking it to the ground, he'd had his best advantage—*size.* But his vanity, his fear of pain had cost him. He was bigger, but she'd trained her whole life. He clearly didn't have a clue how to grapple.

She reversed the pin, now using her hooked arm and leg to pull herself completely out from under him. He tried to squash her again, realizing he was losing his advantage. But it happened too fast. Now she was on top. She didn't hesitate, slipping her other foot around his right side now so she was practically piggy-back riding. He was pushing off the ground, though. The big ones always tried the same thing. They thought they could slam someone to the ground hard enough to dislodge them.

She only had seconds.

Her arm looped around his throat. Her other arm locked it in. She squeezed the rear-naked choke as tightly as she could. Her head pounding, her body aching. She twisted and squeezed as if she were wrangling some rodeo bull, putting her whole force and body behind it.

The man was cursing and spluttering and stumbling.

Behind them another metal suit. Dakota's eyes widened. She was squeezing his throat, but he was trying to slam her against the wall. His size would crush her, even with the choke in place. Not enough time.

So at the last minute she did the only thing she could think of. As he surged backwards, propelling himself *hard* into the wall, she dropped her grip instantly. Legs off, hands off. She fell like a stone and hit the ground.

A silly maneuver, and one that never would've worked in a cage.

But the big man wasn't reacting like a seasoned veteran. He was panicking. She doubted anyone had ever threatened him physically before. She wasn't out of the woods yet, though.

She hit the floor, tucking into a ball. Pain lanced up her knees and hands where she struck. A big foot caught her ribs as the killer stumbled back.

And now he tripped exactly over where she'd fallen.

The momentum from his lunging shove followed by his stumble sent him careening back into his own sculpture. His head struck metal. The metallic construction collapsed with him in a loud *thud.*

The big man groaned once. He held up a hand, staring dazedly at where blood now trickled along his fingers. "Yuck..." he whispered. His eyes fluttered.

He went still.

But Dakota didn't have time to celebrate. "Help!" a voice gasped. "Please—please—he—he..." The voice was struggling for words, struggling, by the sound of things, to even *breathe.*

Dakota whirled and spotted where part of one of the swinging angels had collapsed. Right on top of the woman beneath the metal wicket. Her face was pale, her eyes open and alert now. But she was gasping for air, the metallic, winged creation lodged against her chest, suppressing her lungs.

Dakota cursed, sprinting over. She ripped at the angel, groaning as she tried to lift it. “Help me,” she gasped out. “Count of three. Ready? One... two...” She groaned and the woman beneath the metal piece let out a gasp as she tried to shove as best as she could.

It wasn't much, but together, the two of them were able to push the winged thing a foot to the right. It came crashing down to the floor a second later, but this time—mercifully--not on top of the victim.

Dakota gasped, dropping to the woman's side. “Are you oka—” she began.

But then she heard a loud *thump.* And something struck her across the back of the head *hard*! Dakota hit the ground, trying to catch herself. But her arm wasn't moving well. Her thoughts were sluggish. The black spots across her vision were now white.

She blinked, trying to see. She caught glimpses of a massive shape stooped over her. Speckles of blood tapped against her cheeks, falling from the giant form. She glimpsed the killer leering down at her. A look of rage and grim satisfaction competing across his visage. He held her in place and then, with his bare hands, bent a piece of rebar over her to form another wicket, trapping her arms at her side, trapping her against the ground.

He growled at her. “You'll do,” he said in a whisper. He shook his head, more blood drops flying. Dakota kicked and cursed, but it was far more difficult to adopt half guard against a metal beam.

She struggled, but the metal wouldn't budge. She tried to slip through it, but the man put his foot on her throat. He reached for his blowtorch, heaving a massive sigh. He whispered, “This will only hurt a little.”

The blue flame leapt from the end of the tool, sparking above her. He was grinning now, still bleeding, his eyes truly mad.

Then, he began to lower the flame towards her eyes.

CHAPTER THIRTY TWO

Dakota felt heat against her cheek, as she desperately tried to dislodge her arms from the metal bar the man had bent so easily. But for her it was futile. Her skin warmed beneath the blowtorch. The man above her chuckled in that childish, high-pitched voice of his.

Despair settled on Dakota like a cloak.

And that's when Agent Marcus Clement made his entry. All three hundred pounds of muscle and ill-intent. Marcus slammed into the giant killer from behind, bringing the two of them crashing to the ground in a tangle of limbs.

Marcus shouted, "Dakota! Are you ok—"

But he didn't have time to complete his wellness check on account of the fingers groping at his throat. The two men rolled one way, then the other, knocking over sculptures and art pieces. Marcus hit one of the ellipticals, toppling it. He grabbed a fifty-pound metal plate from the barbell, hefting it like it was little more than a sheet of paper.

Briefly, eyes wide, skin still buzzing, Dakota just stared in awe and amazement. The two enormous men slugged it out. Punching, then rolling, grappling then punching again. There was no technique, no finesse to the motions. Just sheer rage and brawn.

The two of them were now wrestling over a hundred-pound dumbbell weight, both trying to use it to cudgel the other.

Marcus was breathing heavily already. The big agent was an excellent partner in the field, but he didn't have nearly the stamina as the killer. Dakota struggled desperately, cursing and kicking. Finally, with a groan, she managed to slip through the hoop of bent metal, shimmying like a snake.

She pushed to her feet, struggling desperately in Agent Clement's direction. "Marcus!" she shouted in warning.

Clement ducked just in time to avoid being clobbered by another dumbbell. The weight flew through the air, smashed through a blacked-out window and just kept going. A second later there was a loud *crunch* followed by a car alarm.

She winced, wondering if Father Duncan's loaner had just gone for a second round. She wasn't sure how she was going to explain all the damage.

Now, though, her focus was diverted. Marcus was truly struggling now. He'd come in full force, but he was now panting, sweating, still going at it full force but losing pace.

The killer seemed to sense the opening. He was moving faster, forcing the tempo. Both men were bleeding. Both bruised, both with ripped shirts. Marcus threw a haymaker but missed completely now—a sloppy blow.

The killer crowed in delight and punched Marcus in the stomach.

Dakota was on her feet, stumbling towards them, trying to catch her bearings. She was sleep-deprived, bruised, half-crushed, and exhausted. She reached one of the weight racks. She tried to lift the fifty-pound weight, but it was too heavy to wield.

She cursed as Marcus let out a gasp, dropped to the ground by another blow. She grabbed a much smaller, twenty-pound weight and then rushed the killer from behind.

"I purge the small things," he was shouting in Marcus's face. Spittle and blood flecked Clement's cheeks as he tried to push back to his feet. "I purge them—I re-create them. You stare at greatness!" He raised his bludgeoning weapon, preparing to cave Marcus's head in.

Dakota reached him a second before he could move. "No!" she shouted. More out of disagreement than horror. The twenty-pound weight smacked the man across the back of the head, hard.

He wobbled, blinked once, and then collapsed like a sack of bricks between Marcus and Dakota, absolutely motionless.

The two of them stood quiet, both breathing heavily, both staring at the fallen monster.

"Shit," Dakota said.

"Holy shit," Marcus replied. He winced, rubbing at a split lip and pulling fingers away stained with blood.

Dakota pointed at her partner. "Nice timing."

He glanced at the dumbbell in Dakota's two hands, then at the fallen Goliath. "You too. Demiurge. Do you know what that means?"

"No, but I know what shit means. You said it. I heard you. You swore."

"Did not."

Dakota snorted, but was already turning, hastening back towards the fallen victim who was sitting upright, crying, her eyes wide. Clearly, she was in shock.

"Hang on," Dakota said hurriedly. "It's going to be okay," she said.

"You're going to be okay."

The woman blinked, staring at Dakota, tears streaming down her face. Marcus was busy checking on the killer, making sure he was down for the count. Dakota heard the sound of cuffs then a second curse word from the normally self-censoring big man.

"Don't think these are going to fit!" he shouted.

Dakota pulled her own from her hip, tossing them without looking across the room. "Try two!"

She was on a knee again, concern in her eyes as she tended to the woman. A bit of a role reversal, she thought to herself. Normally, Marcus was concerned with the victims. Dakota with the killers.

Or maybe that was just what she liked to tell herself. In as soothing a tone as she could muster, she whispered, "You're going to be okay. It's alright. You're fine. He's done. He's gone."

"Benjamin," she was saying, her voice shaking. "I—I know him from group."

Dakota patted the woman on the arm. "Help is on the way."

She glanced up towards the smashed window. She'd already spotted the flashing red and blue lights. Backup was drawing nearer. "Help is on the way," she repeated, breathlessly, collapsing into a sitting position next to the survivor. "You're going to be fine," she whispered. "Just fine."

CHAPTER THIRTY THREE

Dakota yawned, sitting on the edge of her hotel bed and scratching at the bandage wrapped around her forehead. The loop of gauze had seemed like overkill at the time, but Dakota wasn't complaining.

A full night of sleep did wonders for one's mood.

Agent Clement stood in the doorway to the hotel room, watching her from beneath hooded eyes. This was partially because he kept wincing every time he stepped on his left ankle.

She shifted, zipping her carry-on where she'd stowed the last of her things.

"You good to go?" Marcus asked, wincing again and touching fingers to his split lip. He'd refused stitches for it, citing how he'd never needed them for a busted mouth before.

But Dakota suspected he was simply scared of needles. The two of them were taking their time to leave for the airport and get on a plane back to Quantico. There was something nice about not having to rush.

Dakota inhaled the odor of coffee from the Styrofoam cup in Marcus's hand.

"Where'd you get that?" she said, frowning at the cup.

He pointed towards the floor. "First level."

She whistled. "You were up early."

"Not all of us need as much beauty sleep," he said primly.

She whistled again out of spite. "Funny. But bet you can't do that." A third whistle.

He tried but just winced the moment he pursed his cut lip. He muttered darkly, but his eyes held good humor. As Dakota pushed off the edge of the bed, hefting her carry-on item and bidding farewell to the last known location of a full night's rest, Marcus's expression sobered.

"Did you hear?" he said.

"Huh?"

"She's going to make a full recovery. They even released her from the hospital this morning. She's shaken, but fine."

"Physically fine," Dakota murmured. Still, she smiled at the news.

Marcus beamed back. "There it is—I miss seeing it sometimes."

She stopped smiling.

He rolled his eyes but ended the motion with a shoulder shrug. "Not bad, you know. First case back and all."

"This is my second case back."

"Not reinstated it isn't. It's going to look good to the boss. I already put in a good word. Told her how you handled Zeus all on your own."

"Zeus? I was thinking more like Goliath."

Marcus shrugged. "I think that makes you a Bible character. Super holy." He widened his eyes and put on a high-pitched voice. "Purge them all!" He tried to chuckle but just ended up wincing in pain again.

Dakota rolled her eyes, hefting her bag. "Whatever, Clement. Say—hang on... I'm getting a call. I'll be down in a sec."

Marcus flashed a thumbs up, turning on his heel and moving quickly. "Don't keep 'em waiting. Chicago taxis are notorious."

She waved him away with a forced smile. Once he'd gone, she reached out, shutting the hotel door before answering. She tried to smile to force some color into her voice.

"Hey Coach," she said.

Coach Little's strong Irish brogue returned with, "I missed your call, Tastee... Shoulda called again, I didn't see. An old man could get downright sensitive about neglect. You should know better."

She forced a chuckle. Inwardly, though, she thought about the call she'd never completed. About everything she'd wanted to say. But Coach Little was in another state. He had his own concerns to worry about. Still, it was nice of him to call.

"Sorry about that," she said. "I'll try to keep in touch. Appreciate the call though."

He snorted. "Don't do that."

"Do what?"

"Try to chase me off the line like somehow you're not worth my time."

She blinked. "I—what?"

"You," he said, "are worth my time. You used to call regular. I miss those days. How was the case? How are things? Dammit—gotta get me to beg or what? Kinda selfish Tastee."

She blinked in surprise. Stunned, she felt a lump in her throat. She swallowed, smiling for real now. Her chest prickled with something akin to warmth. "I—oh. Well, good actually. Solved it."

"Ha! Knew you had it in ya!"

"Actually got to use a move you taught me at the gym. You

would've liked the bout."

He let out a cackle and she heard what sounded like his walking stick thumping the ground. "Good shit, Steele. Not that it would've mattered."

"What wouldn't have?"

"If you solved the case or not." He grunted. "Never mattered if you won a bout or lost neither."

She blinked, suddenly awash with memories of Little's gym back in Rapid City. Of the fights she'd had, the training. She felt another lump in her throat and swallowed quickly. "I—yeah I always appreciated that about you," she said. "You really did root for us. All of us. Even when we lost."

"Course I did. I was training fighters. Not prize horses. Part of a complete fighter is losing well." He coughed briefly and she heard him lower the phone and shout at someone in the distance. "...hands up!" he was saying. "No—don't drop the left. He's aiming right for—yeah, there you go! Now do it again!" His voice returned full volume. "Sorry about that. What was I saying?"

"Something about losing."

He snorted. "Take a good look at some of these new whelps in here, Tastee, and you'd realize some of them are *experts* on that subject."

She snorted in laughter but immediately felt bad, remembering just how hard it had been when she'd first started fighting too. She frowned though, considering what he'd said. "Losing well... what does that look like?"

"Obvious ain't it? Not giving up. That's all losing is—an opportunity to quit. Don't. You never did before. I've never trained quitters."

She let out a long sigh, feeling that warmth in her chest spreading now. "No," she said huskily. "I guess not. Thanks for the call, Coach."

"Of course. Of course. Don't be a stranger. Stop by sometime—you can teach a couple of these young'uns a move or two."

"Happily," Dakota said with a grin. In the distance, through the door, she heard Marcus calling for her. She thought she caught the words, "…taxi..." and "...Chicago..."

"Hey, Dakota—last thing."

She paused. "Yeah, Coach?"

"Nice to see you bouncing back. Even if it takes three months, you can always choose to try again. See ya around, bud." He hung up first as was customary for Little.

She rolled her eyes, pocketing her phone, hefting her carry-on and moving towards the hotel door again. When she glanced back, she noticed a small mini-fridge by the bed.

She frowned. She h'dn't even noticed it the night before. She heard Marcus calling up after her. Normally a very patient man, she could tell he was getting antsy.

No one was on the same floor as her. No one would know. 'he'd done well, h'dn't she? She deserved a little reward.

She stared towards the small fridge. Such a strange thought to have had it right next to her head all night, for hours, without even realizing. And now just *knowing* it was there made a difference.

What sort of selection would they have? Just a sip. She w'sn't going to go overboard. Just a little fun... 'he'd caught a killer. 'he'd done well.

She let out a fluttering little sigh, taking a half step back into the room.

But she caught herself, actually planting her hands on either side of the door frame and bracing there.

She frowned. "No," she muttered. The same word 'he'd shouted at the killer. She w'sn't a quitter.

Not today. Maybe never again if she could help it. She stared at the fridge. Losing was one thing—she could come back from a loss. But quitting?

"Hell no," she muttered to herself. She shoved violently out into the hall, slamming the door behind her. And, as silly as it must have looked, she broke into sprint, a dead run, racing away from the hotel door, sprinting towards the stairs and in the direction of Marcus's shout.

"Taxi is going to leave, Dakota! Come on!"

As she ran, and then took the stairs three at a time, feeling both silly and elated, Dakota couldn't help but smile.

EPILOGUE

Things going on here... things you and Marcus never knew. Just let it go...

Dakota replayed the message again, frowning where she sat by the orchids in her living room. The violet flowers were blooming again, slowly. The green buds pressed from the stem where she'd pruned it months before. She'd purchased another one and placed it next to the first. Something about watching the flowers grow gave her apartment, new as it was, a more homey feel.

She stared out the window of her new home, frowning over the blooming flowers as she clicked the replay button. *Things going on here... things you and Marcus never knew. Just let it go...*

The voice of her old supervising agent shook as it spoke. Fear? She couldn't quite place the emotion. Anger? She'd never really questioned why Agent Drafuss had been fired the week after she'd left. Politics at the bureau could be downright brutal.

But now she couldn't help but consider the implications. The killer who'd gotten away months before was still out there. Her old supervising agent was in the wind, his address unlisted now. Either he didn't want to be found, or someone else didn't want him to be found.

And now this voicemail.

Dakota played it again. Determined to memorize the entire thing. She sighed as she lowered her phone, rubbing the bridge of her nose. It was nice to be back in her place, though a bit lonely. Maybe the flowers would do as a start, but a cat? A puppy?

She snorted, wondering what Coach Little would think if he heard her thoughts. Dakota Steele, cat lady.

It had a nice ring to it...

She shook her head, frowning, thinking back to the failed case once more. Every time she considered it, she had that same prickle of anxiety that started in her chest and spread. She was trying to get better at paying attention to her emotions—when she had them. And when they weren't simply from a place of anger.

Forgiveness... What a strange word to hold onto. But that whiteboard back in the church's basement seemed to have her number.

It was living rent-free in her mind, having taken up occupancy amidst her thoughts.

She supposed the reason it had such an impact was because it was right. She couldn't move on without forgiving herself. But over what?

The case?

She tapped her fingers against the table supporting the two orchids. No—not the case. Not *just* the case. Part of her knew, though she didn't want to admit it, that she was fighting a losing battle unless she dealt with where it *all* actually started. Not just the case from three months ago. But the reason she'd made a bad call three months ago.

Blood on a small backpack. A walk home from school ending in tragedy.

Dakota shivered, thinking of how she'd been in detention at the time, unable to escort her baby sister home.

Just as quickly as the recollections came, she shut them off, grinding her teeth in the same way she ground the memories.

Some things just weren't worth dwelling on. She couldn't change the past—that much was certain. But if she wanted to move forward?

She got to her feet, moving towards the shower, feeling the ache in her arms and neck. Moving forward meant looking back. Meant her father... and sister.

She sighed and then on a whim whipped her phone up, moved to the email. She typed in the address bar and stared at the empty screen. She'd solved the case, hadn't she? That had to mean Supervising Agent Carter would stop being such a stick in the mud, didn't it?

She snorted, shaking her head.

If only. People like Agent Carter *enjoyed* the power they held over others. At least, that's how Dakota saw it.

She turned on the freezing water to the shower, watching as the droplets speckled the porcelain. Not as strong of a spray as the shower back home, but it would do. She rolled her shoulders, turning to face the mirror.

She liked the freezing showers. Like practicing shadowboxing beneath the spray. The pain helped her focus. Forced her to stay on task.

A few droplets speckled her skin where she stood next to the shower. Dakota let out a faint huff of air, reaching a final decision.

And then, she began to type.

An information request. She'd make it official. Not information pertaining to the case from three months ago, though. At least not *just* that. Two requests. Both to Agent Carter. One for the case she'd failed and one...

For her baby sister. Another flash of memory. A blood-speckled backpack on the side of the road.

Dakota shivered, hastily pressing send and then slamming her phone into the dish by the sink. She began to undress, anticipating the frigid spray, the refocusing of her mind.

Coach Little was right... Even if it took three months to try again, she wasn't a quitter.

But what if it took more than two decades?

She pushed her head under the water first, feeling the sudden tingle along her scalp, her back muscles tensing against the cold.

Even after two decades, could she try again?

She had to move past it. That much was clear. Her father and her sister. That's where it had all started. Her father, she knew, collected information on the two decade-old case. He compiled it in a red binder he kept by his bed. He'd never stopped—he'd been obsessed. Too obsessed to realize what was happening to his other daughter. Too obsessed to love. Too obsessed to parent.

But he'd collected information for years after the disappearance of Dakota's sister. If anyone had something new, it would be him.

Some skeletons were best left buried in the closet. But now her closet was full.

She reached for her phone, exhaling slowly. Then, she dialed her father's number from memory.

NOW AVAILABLE!

WITHOUT A PAST
(A Dakota Steele FBI Suspense Thriller—Book 3)

MMA champ-turned-FBI Special Agent and BAU specialist Dakota Steele is as tough as they come—and as brilliant, too, able to crack serial killers that no one else can. When a new serial killer appears, using dangerous chemicals to murder victims, it's up to Dakota and her partner to track him down. But this killer is unlike any she's seen before—and Dakota may just find her own life in danger.

"The plot has many twists and turns, but it is the ending, which I did not see coming at all, that totally defines this book as one of the most riveting that I have read in years."
—Reader review for Not Like Us

WITHOUT A PAST is book #3 in a new series by critically-acclaimed and #1 bestselling mystery and suspense author Ava Strong.

Dakota's personal life offers no refuge from the stress. She has finally summoned the courage to contact her father, but their relationship is rocky at best, and Dakota is no closer to finding the answers she needs to unravel the mysteries of her past—and of her sister's disappearance.

Can Dakota stop the killer in time to save the next victim?

Can she find her own sister's killer? Or will her past remain a mystery forever?

A complex psychological crime thriller full of twists and turns and packed with heart-pounding suspense, the DAKOTA STEELE mystery series will make you fall in love with a brilliant new female protagonist and keep you turning pages late into the night.

Future books in the series will be available soon.

“This is a chilling, suspenseful page turner that just might leave you scared at night!”
—Reader review for Not Like Us

“Very intriguing, kept me turning page after page… Lots of twists and turns and a very unexpected ending. Cannot wait for the next in this series!”
—Reader review for Not Like Us

“A roller coaster ride of events… Can’t put down until you finish it!”
—Reader review for Not Like Us

“Excellent read with very realistic characters that you become emotionally invested in… Couldn't put it down!”
—Reader review for The Death Code

“An excellent read, lots of twists and turns, with a surprising ending, leaving you wanting to read the next book in the series! Well done!”
—Reader review for The Death Code

“Well worth the read. Cannot wait to see what happens in the next book!”
—Reader review for The Death Code

“Quickly became a story I couldn’t put down! I highly recommend this book!”
—Reader review for His Other Wife

“I really enjoyed the fast-paced action, plot design and characterization... I didn't want to put the book down and the ending was a total surprise.”
—Reader review for His Other Wife

“The characters are extremely well developed… There are twists and turns in the plot that kept me guessing. An extremely well written story.”
—Reader review for His Other Wife

"One of the best books I have ever read… The ending was perfect and surprising. Ava Strong is an amazing writer."
—Reader review for His Other Wife

"Holy cow, what a rollercoaster… Many times I absolutely KNEW who the killer was—only to be proven wrong each time. I was completely surprised by the ending. I have to say, I am thrilled that this is the first in a series. My only complaint is that the next one isn't out yet. I need it!"
—Reader review for His Other Wife

"An incredible, intense, spellbinding, enjoyable story. It will keep you captivated until the end."
—Reader review for His Other Wife

Ava Strong

Bestselling author Ava Strong is author of the REMI LAURENT mystery series, comprising six books (and counting); of the ILSE BECK mystery series, comprising seven books (and counting); of the STELLA FALL psychological suspense thriller series, comprising six books (and counting); and of the DAKOTA STEELE FBI suspense thriller series, comprising three books (and counting).

An avid reader and lifelong fan of the mystery and thriller genres, Ava loves to hear from you, so please feel free to visit www.avastrongauthor.com to learn more and stay in touch.

BOOKS BY AVA STRONG

REMI LAURENT FBI SUSPENSE THRILLER
THE DEATH CODE (Book #1)
THE MURDER CODE (Book #2)
THE MALICE CODE (Book #3)
THE VENGEANCE CODE (Book #4)
THE DECEPTION CODE (Book #5)
THE SEDUCTION CODE (Book #6)

ILSE BECK FBI SUSPENSE THRILLER
NOT LIKE US (Book #1)
NOT LIKE HE SEEMED (Book #2)
NOT LIKE YESTERDAY (Book #3)
NOT LIKE THIS (Book #4)
NOT LIKE SHE THOUGHT (Book #5)
NOT LIKE BEFORE (Book #6)
NOT LIKE NORMAL (Book #7)

STELLA FALL PSYCHOLOGICAL SUSPENSE THRILLER
HIS OTHER WIFE (Book #1)
HIS OTHER LIE (Book #2)
HIS OTHER SECRET (Book #3)
HIS OTHER MISTRESS (Book #4)
HIS OTHER LIFE (Book #5)
HIS OTHER TRUTH (Book #6)

DAKOTA STEELE FBI SUSPENSE THRILLER
WITHOUT MERCY (Book #1)
WITHOUT REMORSE (Book #2)
WITHOUT A PAST (Book #3)